I0593931

Blood Crystal

Blood Crystal
A novella

Jeanette O'Hagan

Story 2 Under the Mountain series

By the Light Books

Blood Crystal: a novella
By Jeanette O'Hagan
Story 2 in the Under the Mountain series

Cover design: Jeanette O'Hagan © 2017
Typesetting and Layout: Jeanette O'Hagan
Copyright Jeanette O'Hagan © 2017 http://jeanetteohagan.com

NLA Cataloguing-in-Publication entry:

Creator: O'Hagan, Jeanette, author.

Title: Blood crystal : a novella / Jeanette O'Hagan.

ISBN: 9780994398987 (paperback)

Series: O'Hagan, Jeanette. Under the mountain ; 2.

Subjects: Fantasy fiction.

Twins--Fiction.

Cooperation--Fiction.

Courage--Fiction.
ISBN-13: 978-0-9943989-8-7

Published through By the Light Books
By the Light Books PO Box 2520, Brookside Centre, Qld 4053
Email: Bythelightbooks@gmail.com

Note: This book follows Australian style conventions for spelling, punctuation and grammar.

Subscribe to Jeanette O'Hagan's Newsletter for the latest on new releases, giveaways and other news– http://eepurl.com/bbLJKT

Dedicated to my parents,
Thomas Cooper Curtis and Jean Florence Ayles,
who met and married in Mt Isa,
a mining town.

Boom, baboom. Something heavy smashed against the metal doors of Grand Cavern. Delvina braced herself, the stone floor vibrating beneath her boots. This assault from the tunnels beyond the door was longer and more ferocious than the last. She gripped the rim of the basket she was hauling and shuffled closer to her twin, Retza, reassured by his solid presence and the familiar smells of rock dust and mushroom soup on his rough clothes.

Retza pushed his lips into a stiff smile. 'It's going to be okay.'

'Yes, maybe this time.' Delvina swallowed against the sudden tightness in her throat. How long could they withstand the former Overseer Uzza's attacks? Somehow, he'd regrouped with his followers in the abandoned tunnels. Worse, while Old Barekia had repaired the Crystal Heart, it was now producing only half the power. How long before it failed again? How long before food and air dwindled? Cold fear fingered her heart and squeezed the breath from her lungs.

The fug of stale sweat and torch smoke clotted the atmosphere of the huge cavern. The soft whimpering of the youngwuns and the nervous coughs and subdued crying of their carers were barely audible above the thumping of her heart. Prentices and crew scrambled to shore up the defences while the old and injured huddled with youngwuns at the back. The new Overseer, Havilah, her grey streaked hair caught up in a bun, moved among them, bending to speak to an aged whitebeard, to place a comforting hand on the head of a littlewun, to give orders to the leadwuns and defenders. Danel and Nebam flanked her, gripping their newly issued watcher truncheons.

Boom, boom, boom.

The thick metal cavern doors shuddered in front of her. Rock grit drifted from the cavernous ceiling and the bluish glimmer lights flickered overhead.

A large watcher ran past them. 'You prentices, don't dawdle! Get the rubble up to the drop holes.'

With a grunt, Delvina heaved up the basket of rocks and scrap. She headed towards the spiral stairs cut into the rock pillars flanking the shield doors. Retza's heavy steps followed behind her, his breath hot on the back of her neck.

Once at the top of stairs, she jogged along the enclosed logia jutting out over the entrance tunnel to the Grand Cavern's shield doors. She ducked her head to avoid hitting the low uneven roof. Together, she and Retza emptied their baskets on the shrinking piles of rocks, scrap metal, broken tools and other debris beside the defenders.

Through the drop holes, she caught a glimpse of the black garbed attackers in the tunnel beneath. They swung a bronze-headed battering ram against the cavern doors. Rocks and refuse rained down through the drop holes, pinging against makeshift shields and helmets. A rock the size of a fist smashed into an attacker with a plaited blue-dyed beard. With a grunt, he pitched forwards and was trampled by the boots of the other followers of the old Overseer behind him. Another clutched her eye, dark blood streaming down her face. The rest continued with barely a pause, swinging the ram forward. Boom, boom, boom. Again, the door shuddered, the great metal hinges groaning.

She pushed away the thought of what Uzza's followers would do to them, to her, if they broke through the doors into the Cavern. Delvina swallowed against the nausea. She didn't want to think of the flash of the sacrificial knife against young flesh, the gaping hole into darkness in the Sunken Temple. The massive iron doors of the Grand Cavern could withstand multiple attacks, but surely even they had a limit? And what if the old guard found a way to tunnel into the safe areas? They might emerge anywhere within the central shafts.

A tug on Delvina's jerkin jolted her attention back to the logia. Grime and sweat streaked Retza's pale face. His white-gold hair was matted beneath his cap. 'We need to fill the baskets again.'

She bobbed her head, her plait swinging against her back. Pushing down the weary ache in her limbs, she trundled back down the stairs to refill her basket. It was hard to imagine what their new found friend, Zadeki, would be doing in the great outside of burning lights and endless sky. They could do with his help about now. But he was gone, back with his kin and no reason to return so soon. Surely it couldn't end like this?

Golden sunlight filtered between the thick foliage of giant forest trees, painting flickering green shadows on Zadeki's silvery-white skin. He hardly looked to see where he put his feet on the worn path snaking through the Great Forest. No need with his position at the end of the group of pregnant and nursing mothers and anyone else too young or perhaps injured to shapeshift. It wasn't that there was much in all the wide lands that the Forest Folk couldn't defeat if called upon, but they were a peaceful people and those bound to the land were most vulnerable when following the song-lines of the seasons.

High up in the canopy, the brilliant red and green feathers of a macaw flashed in the clear morning light. Zadeki's arms trembled in eagerness for flight forbidden to him. He adjusted the heavy bag of utensils on his back and ground his teeth. It was good to be home after spending half the cycle of the Golden Moon, Alumi, in the dark, claustrophobic tunnels beneath the mountain. But it was frustrating to be in the protected group when he was old enough to at least be an outlier. His broken arm was healed and he'd grasped two major forms of jaguar and eagle already.

He kicked a pebble off the path, watching it bounce and disappear in the thick understory vegetation. Zadeki's dawn meal of fish, nuts and fruit soured in his stomach as he remembered the scathing words of the Kinleader.

'Son of my son's son, you are clearly not ready to be a pathfinder, as your reckless flight across mountains proves. It's a wonder you were not killed. We—'

He'd protested. 'But Kinleader, I helped the earthbiters ...'

His baba gripped his shoulder. 'Hush, son. Don't interrupt the Kinleader.'

With a snap of her grey-green eyes, she continued. 'We lost time in our search for you and will be late to the golden sava-root harvest.' Her severe expression softened a fraction. 'I'm interested in your encounter with the

Darane, Zadeki, but it will have to wait for now. You are grounded six cycles of Golden Moon.'

He'd been too ashamed at the time to argue, though the wide lands were bountiful enough that a few days less digging up the sava roots would hardly mean they'd go hungry. He shifted the straps of the bag and sighed. Maybe the Kinleader had a point. It was by the Maker's favour he'd survived. But it was not so favourable that a snowstorm had blown up out of nowhere and slammed him into the mountain in the first place.

A hand fell onto his shoulder. 'Cheer up little brother. Being a carrier is not the end of the world, you know.'

Zadeki shrugged off Josenif's hand and continued walking with his head down. It was all very well for his eldest brother to say so. He had been a pathfinder for many cycles of the sun's song.

'I know it seems like ages but give it time, young Zadeki. You'll get your chance to prove yourself.' Josenif's cheerful face split into a grin, his forest-green eyes crinkled at the corners. He twirled a twig in his hands. 'You take things too intensely.'

'Nice to know I'm a joke to the rest of my family. That gives me comfort.' Zadeki twisted around and scowled at his brother. 'I'm not a youngling anymore. That snowstorm came out of nowhere. Even you couldn't have done anything about it.'

'Sudden changes in weather are to be expected in the mountains. A pathfinder knows how to read the signs, a wise one doesn't travel alone.' Josenif waggled his dark eyebrows.

Zadeki glared at him. Their eyes now level since his recent growth spurt but, somehow, he still felt small beside his older, more experienced brother. 'How can I learn, stuck at the back of the land-bound column carrying the baggage?'

'Listen, scamp. We couldn't find you. Don't you know how worried Matu and Baba were? When we could find no trace of you for over fifteen days? You broke your arm. It's a wonder that you survived on the heights.'

'But I did survive.' And helped save the tunnel dwellers too. Would they believe in his amazing tale of the deep caverns and the mad Overseer? Maybe Josenif would. Sometimes he wondered if he dreamt it all in some injured haze.

'The point is, you should've been doing your assigned task, and you should never fly in the mountains alone. Until you learn to work as part of a team, you're not ready to be a pathfinder.'

Zadeki tensed. He expected the lectures from the Kinleader, from Matu and Baba and his uncles and aunts, but not from his favourite older brother. He turned his head away. 'Now you sound like the Kinleader.'

Josenif chuckled. 'It's just common sense, scamp. You'll get your chance one day.'

Zadeki kicked another pebble out of his way. A lizard scuttled up the rough bark of a seiba tree. Yes, and how long would that take? He almost wished he was back in the Darane's dreary tunnels with Delvina and Retza. They treated him with respect, well at least by the end. Being back in the closed-in, stuffy darkness with his earthbiter friends was better than being grounded.

The whisper of furtive footsteps woke Delvina. The lights in the huge cavern were dimmed for the late shift and the smooth rock floor was covered with mounds of sleeping people. It was hours since the attack had been repulsed, yet the leadwuns hadn't yet released the people to their cribs. Not until the watchers had done a sweep of the outlying tunnels to ensure the Old Guard had retreated with their wounded to whatever deep abandoned pit they were hiding in. Only those who had active shifts in the mine shafts could leave. Delvina was so bone weary, she hadn't minded where she slept, but questions about the fading Crystal Heart ate away at her like acid on freshly mined ore. She had to get answers.

A dissonant medley of snores, coughs and heavy breathing filled the dim space. The muffled sound of footsteps and a shadow flickering against the wall caught her attention. Nebam and Danel picked their way across to the door leading to the mountain's Heart, the power room. The soft sibilant sounds of their conversation sighing from the passageway. It seemed she wasn't the only one that couldn't sleep. A few moments later, Putarn followed, head thrust forward as he stumped past and disappeared through the doorway.

Delvina rolled over and shook her brother.

'Wha ... Is it time for our shift? Another attack?' Retza sat up, scratching his stomach and yawning.

She wrinkled her snub nose. 'I think Overseer Havilah is having a council meeting. Maybe they are discussing the glimmer lights situation.'

Retza's pale eyes cleared of sleep in an instant. 'Let's find out, then.'

In unison, they belted their tunics and pulled on their thick, felt cloaks.

Delvina eyed her studded boots. 'Best leave those.'

Retza nodded. 'The quieter the better.'

Delvina followed Retza as he crept between the

sleeping bodies and slipped into the corridor. Once they reached the three-way junction, they took the right turn towards the Glimmer Heart Room.

The door to the power room was ajar, still waiting to be fixed from when they'd jimmied it open to get to the Crystal Heart over two rosters ago. Scrybe Barekia's frail voice echoed in the passageway. Retza put a thick finger to his lips and they crouched behind the broken door.

'This is beyond my ken, Overseer. As far as I can see the connections are all working. It is as if the crystals themselves are losing their innate power. Maybe some of the other scrybes or old lead hands could help us.'

Delvina clamped her hand to her mouth, smothering a gasp. Then it was more serious than the watchers were making out. If Barekia was worried ...

Havilah's pleasant voice sounded strained and weary. 'Barekia, you are the most knowledgeable oldwun we have.'

'There might be another way to power the crystals.' The harsher voice was Putarn, the leader's second in command and eldest son. Unlike his mother, he liked throwing his weight around, as Delvina knew well enough. He'd made their first days with the Greenstone South Crew difficult.

'What way, Putarn?' Havilah's voice was strained. 'True, we found a large store of coal in Uzza's chambers, along with stuff I haven't seen since I was a youngwun. We can use that for heat and as fuel to cook, but the fumes can be noxious and may poison the air if we're not careful. Besides, it's the glimmer lights that concern me. We need them for the mushroom and potato farms and to power the ventilation shafts.'

"If we could get outside to the mountain valleys ...'

Barekia's voice was hesitant, as if she hardly believed it was an option.

'Our attempts to breech even the first layer of locks, traps and wards on the Mountain Gate cost the lives of all who tried. Without Uzza's seal ...'

'So, if we tunnel...' It was Havilah's second son, Nebam's gruff voice. 'Or hunt Uzza down to whatever lair he's hiding in and wrest the seal off him.'

'And walk right into an ambush or trap? Smart thinking, little brother.'

'By the pit, Putarn, I'm not a youngwun or sparse-bearded prentice. No need to mock me.'

'So, you call that patchy straggle a beard?'

'You can talk. You—'

'Stop it! Just stop it!' Havilah's voice roared with the force of an underground river. 'The situation is serious enough without you squabbling like littlewuns. We need to pull together ...'

Tuning out the lecture, Delvina put her mouth close to Retza's ear. 'Time to return to the Grand Cavern.'

Retza nodded and eased out behind the door, keeping close to the wall. The stomp of studded boots sounded in the tunnel in front of them. Uncertain torchlight sent shadows skittering over the wall. Too late to escape. Delvina caught Retza's arm, jerking him back into the deeper shadow behind the door.

'Hey, what are you youngwuns doing here?' The tall guard Delvina had seen in the cavern earlier in the day grabbed them by the nape of their jerkins and pulled them into the centre of the tunnel. By his height and weight and confident bearing, he looked like a former watcher under Uzza.

'We ... er...' Retza swallowed.

'We thought we heard something,' Delvina offered, then bit her lip. Surely, she could have thought of something better than that. Inside the sounds of argument from the Heart Room stopped abruptly.

'Save your weak-as-water excuses for the Overseer.' The tall watcher jabbed Delvina in the small of her back with his truncheon, prodding her and Retza through the open door.

The Heart Room was large, though still only a third the size of the Great Meeting Cavern. A cluster of massive copper-green crystals stood in the centre of the room. The faceted sides glowed softly in the darkness, throwing patterns over the upturned faces of the small group clustered around it. Brass cogged wheels, pistons and wires hummed in the apparatus around the crystals. Yet their light was less penetrating than the dazzling radiance when Barekia had fixed the Crystal Heart—just a couple of ten-days before.

Havilah turned around, her mauve eyes wide with surprise. She planted a clenched fist on one hip. 'What's this? I said I wasn't to be disturbed.'

'I found these two troublemakers listening outside the door, your Honour.' The guard shoved both Delvina and Retza deeper into the room.

Putarn growled, his cheeks flushed, no doubt from Havilah's scolding. 'Typical from those two. Such behaviour shouldn't be tolerated.'

The Leadwun's lips tightened to a thin line. 'If it weren't for these two, Uzza would have sacrificed the best of the youngwuns and prentices to the Dark Ones.' Her rich voice seemed weighed down with the fatigue of sleepless nights and hard decisions.

Putarn's narrow face distorted into a snarl and he

fingered his scrappy beard. 'Mad as he is, have you thought that Uzza may have been right? What if young blood is necessary to power the Crystal Heart?'

Delvina sucked in a breath. Retza stiffened beside her.

The old Scrybe stopped fiddling with the knobs on the panel below the crystals, and scowled at the Secondwun. 'Nonsense. As if forcing the sacrifice of innocents is a valid solution to any problem.'

Nebam's pale eyes were as wide as two moons in the outside's sky. 'You can't be suggesting—'

'Don't be daft, brother. Not our youngwuns, not even these two. Didn't Uzza leave some of his brats behind in his haste to escape?'

Havilah sliced the air with her hand. 'That's enough, Secondwun! Such absurdity is not happening on my shift. Do I make myself clear?'

'But, if things were desperate? Like you said, after Baba died in … in the mine-collapse, sometimes a few die to save the many.'

Delvina's heart jumped and tears pricked her eyes. Retza moved closer and gripped her arm. Their parents had been killed in that accident so many years ago. Now she sometimes found it hard to remember their faces or the sound of their voices.

A look of pain and grief flashed across Havilah's face, but she didn't look away from her son. 'It's not the same. Your father died a hero.'

Putarn's defiant gaze held a second more before shifting to his scuffed boots. 'Yes, Overseer, so he did.'

Havilah studied the Secondwun before giving a nod. She turned to the tall watcher, standing near the door—silent and grim.

'Thanks for your vigilance, Gilarth. Are the perimeters clear?'

'Yes, your Honour. The crews on late shift are collapsing the old tunnels to the north, though finding them all will take days, maybe longer.'

'Keep at it, man. If we can trap Uzza's forces in the old workings long enough, they will run out of food and supplies.' Her amethyst eyes swept over the twins. 'Leave these two with me.'

The gruff watcher saluted and left the chamber.

Delvina wiped a tear from the corner of her eye and moved closer to Retza. Growing up as orphans, it had just been the two of them until Havilah had taken them into her crew. Delvina wanted to help her leadwun, but maybe the Overseer wouldn't see it that way. Would she demote them to the cesspits or put them on double shifts for snooping on conversations not meant for their ears?

Overseer Havilah ran a hand over her grey-streaked hair. 'What am I going to do with you two?'

Old Barekia put down a wrench. 'You need some more messengers.'

Havilah gave a weary smile, her eyes softening. 'An idea with some merit. Come, join us.' She beckoned to the twins. 'We were just about to break for a meal.'

Retza's stomach grumbled as Danel served out the rations—half a bowl of thin mushroom soup and one algae cake set down in front of each one at the makeshift table. Havilah nodded her thanks and indicated with a wave that the twins should eat. In the last two rosters, worry lines had etched themselves between the eyebrows of their old crew-leader's face.

Barkeia, Nebam and Danel tucked into their food, while Putarn sat to one side, throwing disgruntled looks at the twins.

Overseer Havilah waved a hand. 'How is it with you two? How is Amris working out as the new Greenstone South Lead Hand?'

Retza thrust out his bottom lip. 'Very well, thank you, your Honour.'

He dipped the metal spoon into the aromatic soup, torn between plying the new Overseer with questions and slurping the soup up to the last drop. The opportunity to get answers mightn't come again and Barekia's disclosures were worrying.

Overseer Havilah gave a pained smile. 'I hope the Greenstone South Crew are keeping its morale up despite the attacks. You should tell your shift-mates and all who will listen that we will deal with former leader, Uzza, and his misguided Old Guard followers.'

Retza shifted his position on the stone stool, unsure what to say. It was clear that Uzza was only part of the problem.

Next to him, Delvina leaned forward, her pale grey eyes intense. 'Yes, your Honour. I'm sure you will. But what about the Crystal Heart and the glimmer lights. Shouldn't we be looking for a way out of the cav— ' He kicked his twin under the table before she could say the forbidden words. Delvina sucked in her breath and glared at him.

He glared back before touching his forehead with his knuckle. 'We're loyal subjects, your Honour. My sister Delvina is just a bit excited at times.'

The corners of the leader's mouth tugged upwards. 'As I know, Prentice Retza. I appreciate your caution. However, unlike Uzza, I'm not the Overseer to ban any talk of the outside. Indeed, our finest rock-singers and scrybes are looking for the best places and methods to tunnel outwards—but it could take many roster periods, maybe even solars, before we manage it.

Delvina put down her spoon and took a deep breath, her face intense. 'What about the Cauldron, your Honour. If we can climb the shafts, surely we could climb the walls. We could build stairs or construct a glimmer lift.'

A hush fell on the small group. After a few moments, the Scrybe Barekia spoke. 'The Cauldron opens up far too close to the mountain peaks. No way we could get all the people up there and then down the descent from the heights to the warmer levels. The trek would be deadly.'

Retza shivered, remembering the mounds of cool fluffy white stuff, snow Zadeki had called it, piled up in the Cauldron when he and Delvina had found the above-grounder. Old Barekia had been the first to suggest rebelling against Uzza and fixing the Crystal Heart. She was the one who never gave up. If the old Scrybe thought it was impossible, then perhaps it was.

Barekia pushed aside her bowl, her seamed face set with determination. 'We have to find out why the glimmer crystals are dying and restore their power.'

'And how do you expect to do that, if you haven't already?' Putarn spat out the words as though he'd swallowed splintered bat bones.

Delvina leant forward, gripped Retza's arm. 'Maybe Zadeki's people could tell us.'

Suddenly everyone was speaking over each other, words tumbling like a rock slide.

'Hush.' The Scrybe held up a frail hand, fingers knotted at the joints. When even Putarn had fallen silent, she spoke. 'I did find something that might help.'

'So why didn't you tell us already,' Putarn growled.

'Because you were too busy fighting with your brother. Besides ...' Her voice faded.

Barekia stood and picked up a metal box, placed it on the table and lifted the lid. Retza leaned forward to see this marvellous object. She lifted out a cloth-wrapped shape and, with slow reverent movements, unwrapped it.

A book.

Retza let out his breath between pursed lips, disappointed, not sure what he'd expected. A stone of power, a crystal, a weapon or tool. But it was none of those things, just a book and not a particularly impressive one at that. The leather cover was plain and torn and blackened in places.

The tip of her tongue touching her withered lips, Barekia opened the cover to reveal leaves of yellowed paper covered with a black uneven scrawl. The pages were ripped and marred and looked more fit for tinder than the care Barekia was giving it.

'What is it?' Havilah asked.

'An ancient codex. I found it in the rubble of Uzza's quarters. I think it is a manual for the operation of the Crystal Heart—it has helped, but I'm not sure of the meaning of some of the words, others are missing.'

Reverently, she flipped over several pages before her chipped fingernails stabbed at the text.

'This section talks about the source of power for the Crystal Heart. It draws heat from the rocks deep beneath us but to work properly it has to be in alignment.'

'Alignment with what?'

'That's the question.' Old Barekia shook her white head. 'This phrase might say, but I'm not sure.' She sounded out the words. 'To the chosen shepherd attune, to red heart's beat vibrating, and in true seed's crimson ikor replenished.'

'What does 'ikor' mean?' Retza asked. 'Do we need a plant from the aboveground?'

'Zadeki might know,' his sister said. Her answer for just about anything these days.

Scrybe lifted a scrawny shoulder. 'Prentice Delvina is right. The Forest Folk, the children of starshine, might know the meaning of these words, but we have no way to get to them.'

'The Forest Folk, Zadeki's people.' Delvina tilted her head. 'Retza and I could do it. We could climb the Cauldron, find the forests, find Zadeki and his family and ask them.'

Retza shook his head, the algae cake sinking in his stomach like ballast. Some parts may be scalable, but the sheer walls of the Cauldron were at least a thousand tanis high. 'That's just crazy. No one's done it before.'

The Overseer placed her hand on Delvina's shoulder. 'That's a brave offer, but Prentice Retza is right. No one that I know of has scaled the walls of the Cauldron. Zadeki said he'd return. In the meantime, you are needed here, as messengers.'

Relief spread through Retza's limbs and pleasure at the new appointment. The thought of journeying into the vastness of the outside paralyzed him with fear. Yet, deep down, he couldn't help wondering if maybe his sister was right.

Retza hurried through the dim passages, anxious to re-join Delvina. He'd spent the first shift running errands for the Overseer Havilah, the last errand taking him to the near abandoned rooms of the old Overseer. The glimmer lights seemed dimmer than a few days ago, the air staler, the faces of the watchers and toolwuns grimmer. They were trapped like moths in a cave spider's sticky web, their struggles to escape a certain end binding them tighter.

Retza's footsteps echoed down deserted corridors. He gripped the message cylinder and increased his pace. There had to be a way out of their predicament, another solution, but what? As close as he was to his sister, even he had to admit she sometimes had crazy ideas—ideas like climbing the sheer cliffs of the Cauldron. Nebam's suggestion of digging a tunnel out was the most feasible, but that would take time, more time than he suspected they had. And Delvina's idea that the Old Guard could tunnel into the protected central levels set him on edge.

Retza tried not to think about it. Havilah and the other leadwuns would figure it out.

A loud crash echoed down the passageway ahead of him. He stood still, his heart thudding at the sudden fright. The dim shadows in the long corridor looked empty. Maybe, it was no more than cave rats scavenging in one of the abandoned rooms in the old Overseer's quarters, though it would be a wonder they'd escaped the cooking pots. He shifted the weight of his pack and broke into a jog.

He took only a few strides when a high-pitched cry, a woman's or perhaps a child's voice, came from the same direction as the crash. Then a scrape and the clatter of what sounded like crates being moved. The noises came from a side passage only paces ahead. Blast, it couldn't be rats. The skin at the back of his neck crawled. He hadn't thought anyone was still stationed in these rooms since the old Overseer had fled.

Retza gripped the lift-bar attached to his belt, his fingers tingling. He should report this to the watchers, to Gilarth. Slowing his pace, he took care his boots made no noise as he edged past the side tunnel.

'Take your hands off me, you slag heap! I wouldn't ...' The unseen woman's voice started low and slid up the scale to a piercing screech. 'Don't touch me!'

A deep-throated laugh. 'Who's gonna stop me? Your baba?'

Retza stood still as if his feet were hot metal smelted to the stone. The reddish glare of a rag torch bled on the smooth floor, slashed by long leaping shadows. This didn't sound like a sneak attack of the Old Guard. What was he walking into to? Maybe it was none of his concern.

The thwack of hand against flesh, then more crashes of things falling. 'You she-bat. I'll kill you.'

'You wouldn't dare. I'm ... ow!'

'Leave my sister alone, you bully.' Another voice, definitely a child's.

More scuffling, a thud, a childish wail of pain.

He had to act, he only hoped he didn't regret it. In a rush of adrenalin-charged energy, Retza released the lift-bar from his belt, kicked open the door and scanned the room.

At the back of a dim, medium-sized storeroom, an angular watcher in black bat-leather grappled a young woman, his red face contorted in rage. The woman's fine cotton dress was ripped at the bodice, her pale copper hair spilling down over her shapely shoulders.

A small child, a boy, crouched in the corner among discarded and broken crates, clutching his arm, his lips white.

There were no mounds of rock and dirt, no hole in the floor, no Old Guard marauders. Whatever was going on, this wasn't an invasion.

The watcher had a tight grip on the young woman's wrists, and he seemed unaware of her attempts to stamp on his booted feet and kick his shins. She was too skinny to be beautiful, but she had spirit. The woman's soft blue eyes shone with tears.

She lurched sideways attempting to pull away from her captor. 'Let me go, you oaf.'

Retza took a step back, his neck muscles cording, his chest tightening. This wasn't right but how could he defy a watcher? He shook his head. Idiot. This wasn't the old regime anymore. Havilah would never approve of such predatory behaviour. He'd defended himself against two watchers at once in the battle for the Heart Room.

He took a deep breath of stale air, stepped into the room and raised the lift-bar. 'Do as she says. Let her go.'

The watcher's gaze snapped to his direction. He snarled. 'Get out of here, this is none of your business, slug.'

Retza would know that squashed nose anywhere. Javot had been one of the biggest bullies when he and Delvina were among the crewless struggling for a living in the Commons. When Delvina reported that Putarn was appointing anyone as watchers, even crewless, Retza hadn't believed it. Seems it had been true.

Javot sniggered. 'Don't you know who this is? These are the old Overseer's brats, the ones he left behind.' He twisted the girl's arm. 'Not so high and mighty now, are you, my little jewel.'

Was she truly Overseer's Uzza's daughter? Retza gulped and gripped his lift-bar, too stubborn to back down. 'I said let her go.'

Javot's face took on a calculating look, his pink eyes narrowed to slits. 'Look, you can have a turn after I've ...'

With two strides Retza thwacked the guard over the

shoulders, with the aim to stun rather than kill.

Javot staggered, let go of the girl, twisted and slammed his knee into Retza's leg, missing his groin.

Pain radiated down from Retza's thigh. He gasped for air and struggled to stay upright. Another blow slammed into the side of his head. He shook it against the sudden cascade of sparkling lights and the unwanted memories of being beaten up by Javot when he and Delvina had first arrived in the Commons. His fingers tightened on the lift-bar. He swung it, blocking his tormenter's next blow. The metal bar landed with a sickening crack.

The watcher's face drained of blood as he clutched his arm. 'You'll regret attacking a watcher, slag worm.'

The young woman stepped up behind Javot and brought a clay chika pot down on his head. With a grunt, the watcher collapsed to the ground, blood welling up from cuts in his scalp.

The girl rubbed her hands. 'Not as much as you will.'

Retza pressed his fingers over his bruised cheek. 'Was that necessary? I had him.'

The young woman scrambled backwards to the corner. She scooped the small cowering boy into her arms. Tears tracked down his dirt-smudged face. Leaning forward, she grabbed a splintered slat from off the smashed crates and waved it at Retza.

Since Uzza's father had shut the realm to the outside, even a scrap of wood was precious. While most of the people were on short rations, Uzza and his family had wallowed in luxury. If she was anything like her father, in her fine cotton dress … revulsion and the desire to hurt soured his initial attraction.

'Keep back.' She edged toward the open door.

He gripped the lift-bar harder, then loosened it.

Taking out his anger on her for her father's crimes would not solve anything.

'I won't hurt you, lady, unless you attack me. I'm Retza, Prentice of the Greenstone South Crew and Overseer Havilah's Messenger.'

Her arms wavered and she stiffened them, keeping the sharp point of the wood aiming at him. 'Why should I trust you? You're all savages.'

Retza's cheeks burned. She had all the haughtiness of the highwun, just like Uzza. He spat at the ground in front of her. 'Your father is the savage. He would have sacrificed my sister to ...'

'It was necessary.'

Retza snorted 'No it wasn't. Barekia restarted the Glimmer Heart without the bloodletting.'

'Right, and how well is that working out now? When my baba comes back, he'll fix the glimmer lights properly and you'll all regret mistreating us.'

'And what if it was your ...' His gaze snagged on the young boy in her arms. '... brother whose blood was required?'

Her eyes narrowed then widened. 'Don't be ridiculous.' She backed towards the door he'd entered. The boy sobbed, clinging to her neck. 'Don't follow me, and I won't hurt you.'

A shadow loomed behind her. Gilarth stood at the doorway, his sharp brows wrinkled in a ridge over his deep set, bronze-coloured eyes. 'What's going on here.'

The Overseer's daughter spun around, her gaze locking onto the guard before looking at the floor.

Retza swallowed hard and lowered his lift-bar. 'Javot was attacking the girl. I told him to stop, but he refused ...' Where did this man's loyalties lie? The girl seemed to know him.

'Quite the hero, Prentice Retza. Maybe I should recruit you to the Guard.' Gilarth knelt beside the groaning bully, his lips curled as though he'd eaten days old snails.

Javot spat out some blood. 'This scum Retza was helping the Overseer's brats escape.'

'Strange, I thought you were guarding them.' Gilarth stood up, 'Are you unharmed, Lady Zara?'

'That lout.' She stretched a shaking arm to point at the groaning watcher on the floor. 'That scum promised to help me and then broke Jesson's arm and ...' she swallowed hard, '... almost raped me.' The young woman's eyes were like cold metal as they rested on Gilarth. 'Though why would a traitor like you care? Maybe you put him up to it.'

Gilarth lifted his chin, his face as emotionless as stone. 'I apologise, Lady. Havilah promised to keep you and your brother safe.' He turned to Retza. 'Tie up this fool of a watcher, and then we'll find Barekia or one of the healers. We need a better way to keep these two out of trouble.'

'Hold still.'

Delvina swiped the wet cloth across Retza's cheek and nose. The skin was already purpling, but there didn't seem to be too much damage. Just like Retza to get himself into a patch fight. The initial relief at finding out that her twin was okay, was rapidly being swallowed up by her irritation that he'd put himself in danger. Though, it had been brave of him to defend the girl, even if she was Uzza's daughter.

'Why did you attack Watcher Javot?' Putarn stood

just a pace away, his mauve eyes hard and flat with annoyance. 'Are you an Old Guard sympathiser?'

Gilarth and Nebam stood behind him, their gaze fixed on Retza. At the other end of the meeting room, Barekia was splinting the Jesson's arm while his sister hovered over them. Two watchers stood at the door.

Retza pushed Delvina's hands away and stood up. 'Javot was forcing himself on her. I didn't know who she was, but even so, she doesn't deserve that.'

Putarn mashed his lips together and thrust his face closer. 'Javot says Uzza's brats were trying to escape and that you were helping them.'

'He's a liar.'

'Really ...'

'Don't be foolish, Putarn.' Barekia called out as she eased the child, Jesson, back on to the pallet and gave him a soothing drink.

Putarn twisted around. 'Gamma, he attacked a watcher.'

'And if it wasn't for Retza's refusal to accept Uzza's sacrifice of his sister, that madman would still be in charge.'

Zara's head jerked up and she glared at Retza, her eyes like blue acid. Delvina shivered. She was glad the old Overseers' daughter wasn't looking at her like that.

Gilarth cleared his throat. 'Secondwun, the Scrybe makes sense. Javot used the girl's desire to escape to take advantage of her. He had charge of her. Perhaps, he is the one you should be questioning.'

Putarn's pale face tightened, his mouth twisting. He walked over and stood in front of the tall watcher, tipping his head back. 'Uzza's brats are your responsibility, Head Watcher Gilarth. I suggest you maintain a better hold on them.'

'Point taken, Secondwun. Nevertheless, I suggest Javot be disciplined for his actions.'

Putarn hesitated. He waved a hand. 'I leave that to your discretion. As for Uzza's brats, I want them in a secure room and under the guard of four watchers at all times—'

Gilarth thrust his jaw forward, big hands gripped tight on his truncheon. 'My watchers are stretched thin maintaining the perimeters, guarding those collapsing the tunnels, keeping the core facilities safe ... sir!'

Putarn took a step back, his mouth twisting. 'My matu ... Overseer Havilah ... has decided to put great trust in you, despite your past services to Uzza. I will overlook your failure to maintain control of those under you this time, but if her trust is again betrayed.' His eyes swept the small cavern taking in Gilarth, Nebam, Uzza's children, Retza and coming to rest on Delvina. 'I will deal with you as you deserve.'

Delvina squirmed at the challenge in the Secondwun's eyes, as though she and Retza were troublemakers and he welcomed the chance to reprimand them. Gilarth was right. If anyone was it fault here, it was that bully Javot. Retza had only tried to help.

Zadeki lashed the vine ropes around the last of the temporary platforms. He blinked at the glare of lightning, silver lines snaking through the dark clouds. Moments later, the drawn out rumble of thunder echoed through the dense trees. The smell of rain on leaves and ground, a sudden rush of wind, and the water came sluicing down out of the bruised sky. Laughing, he shimmied up the bamboo pole and dove under the cover of interlaced palm branches.

The afternoon storm was a relief after the oppressive heat building up during the day. Soon the streams and rivers would be running high and they'd move on again, following the plentiful gifts of the Forest. Every day was a new adventure and the thought of staying in one place, living under thick rock as the Darane did, or in dark cold stone houses as the Filane did, was hard to fathom.

His older brothers, Josenif and Benjim, had a small fire going on the fire-guard in the centre of the platform. He inhaled the aromas of the sava root cakes and a small python roasting in the glowing coals. The cooking smells were all the more appetising with the sudden cool from the rain.

'Don't know about you two, but I'm starving.' Josenif rubbed his stomach in exaggerated drama and grinned.

Zadeki moved closer, ready to snag something to eat before his brothers beat him to it.

Benjim pushed him aside. 'Hey, stop dripping on the food—and me. You've been at the camp all day. Besides, you know how hungry shapeshifting makes us.'

'Yeah, ravenous.' Zadeki tried to smile but failed, his good mood suddenly doused as effectively as if it had been left out in the rain. Did Benjim have to point out that he was still grounded. He wanted to ask what his brothers had seen, flying above the forest canopy, but being consigned to grubbing in the mud for roots or slashing bamboo, vines and palm leaves to build shelters for the kin group smarted.

He turned away and stared past the open walls of the shelter to the white-grey curtains of rain, drenching and obscuring the dense green of the understory plants. The clouds lit up with long snakes of lambent silver. Thunder crashed about them.

'Oh, by the way younger brother,' a hand clapped his shoulder. 'The Kinleader wishes to talk to you.'

'Why didn't you say so?' At last he could tell his story. Zadeki jumped up and swung across to the next platform, and the next, making his way to the Kinleader's shelter.

'Scamp, wait until the storm is over,' Josenif shouted after him.

But Zadeki couldn't wait.

Zadeki swung himself into the larger, central shelter. At the far end, the Kinleader was munching on berries and talking in low tones to Baba and one of his great-aunts and a handful of the other elders. She shot Zadeki a quick, frowning glance before turning back to her entourage. Zadeki stood to one side, using the free edge of his white wrap-around sarum to wipe the rain off his face and the leaf litter plastered to his calves and ankles. Maybe Josenif was right, he should have waited for the storm to pass over. He settled down, cross-legged on the rattan mat, closed his eyes, stilled his mind and waited.

The rain came with less force, the lightning and thunder moving to the west and the mountains. A lone bird let forth with an arpeggio, soon joined by others. The rustles of small creatures moving among the underbrush and in the aerial highways merged with the staccato, drip, drip, of water slipping off broad green leaves. The soft murmur of voices faded.

'Son of my son's son, come here.'

He stood, allowing the blood to flow into his stiffened limbs, and approached the Kinleader.

'Da-Matu. Josenif said you wished to speak to me.'

'And so, you immediately charge off here in the middle of a cloudburst like a peccary after sava roots.' The Kinleader smiled. Her grey-green eyes crinkled and her tone held amusement with only a pinch of irritation. She waved her hand. 'Sit down, before I crick my neck.'

He bowed his head and sat, biting down on the urge to explain his enthusiasm. In the tunnels, he had bided his time, waiting for the right opportunity to escape. He could find patience and restraint now. He felt the Kinleader's eyes on him, felt her search his surface emotions but he waited for her to reveal her purpose or give him permission to speak. He resisted the urge to fidget, to shuffle, to explain.

The sun slid out from behind the thick clouds, turning the water droplets on the leaves into a thousand flashing diamonds. Nearby, a baby crowed in pure delight, young children called out laughing and a young woman sang the digging song, the others joining in.

'Tell me about your adventures among the Darane. Don't leave anything out.'

He grinned. At last. And he did as she told him, at first stumbling over the words, not sure how to start, but as she and the elders listened with full attention, not interrupting or questioning, he told them of his injuries, of the twins and the crib, the Overseer Uzza and the Dark Ones and how he and the Greenstone South Crew had stopped the mad leader's terrible plans.

The Kinleader and Baba exchanged glances when he'd finished.

Baba stroked his chin, his face troubled. 'We have not had contact with the mountain dwellers for over two hundred song cycles of the sun.'

'Indeed, Overseer Hezikah, Uzza's father, broke off

contact following a dispute with the Sea Dragon King.

'And now the white ships are slow in coming.' This from his Great-Aunt Bikan. 'But the Darane are not our concern, surely. It was their decision to shut themselves off from the world.'

Baba tilted his head. 'Zadeki did right to help them. They are in a dire situation.'

Zadeki sat straighter, feeling a warm glow at his father's words. 'They want to find the way out, but this Hezikah has blocked the entrance.'

'But you say they have repaired their Crystal Heart. If they have survived two hundred years shut up in the caverns, they can surely survive another,' Bikan said.

An elder from the Mist Forest kin-group nodded. 'We don't want to set the Vaane against us. We decided it was best to keep out of other people's affairs.'

There was a murmur of agreement among the other elders except for Baba. The Kinleader would likely do nothing without the consensus of the elders. This was the way of the Forest Folk, but Zadeki clenched his fists, certain that his new friends needed their help now.

'What if they ask us?' he blurted out.

The Kinleader smoothed her tari across her knees, a fine gold thread through the soft weave catching the sunlight. 'This bears for more thought. As Leader Bikan says, the Darane have survived and will while the Crystal Heart beats. Yet, it would be good to restore our friendship with them.'

Bikan leaned forward. 'What can they do against the Sea Dragon King's troops? We do not want to jeopardise our treaty with the Lonely Isles.'

Da-Matu held up a hand. 'Is friendship a matter of barter, only about what good it does us? I doubt the

Vaane will see this as breaking trust. Besides, we have held them off before, we could do so again, if needed.'

'The Filane, Tamrak's progeny, might stand with us this time,' Baba said.

'Perhaps, my son's son, you have the fire of the koraktil in your veins.' The Kinleader smiled. 'As there is no urgency, we will not rush into a decision. I'll call an elders-meet to discuss the matter at Fang Rock at the next full orb of the Silver One.'

Zadeki supressed a groan. 'But Kinleader, that's a couple of ten-days away.' Maybe even longer as opinions were bandied back and forth until all agreed on a way forward.

'So it will.' The Kinleader smiled at him. 'And perhaps it would be wise to send some pathfinders to the White Mountains to scout out the situation.'

Zadeki grinned. 'I'll go.'

'You are not a pathfinder yet and you are grounded, remember. I will send Josenif and a companion of his choice.'

His shoulders slumped. Though, he could fly back to the mountain realm on his own. The hairs on the back of his neck prickled. He looked up, the Kinleader's eyes were on him. He lifted his chin, meeting her gaze.

'If you promise, young firebrand, to stay with the kin-band and not wander, you may join the foraging group. You will be permitted to shapeshift. And I promise, we seriously consider the plight of the Darane.'

A thrill ran through him. No longer grounded. Was that enough? What of his friends? The Kinleader was fair, and Baba had argued for them. If he went off on his own now, what could he achieve? And if something happened to him, he would most likely turn his Kin against the idea of helping the earthbiters. He would hold the Kinleader to her promise. He wouldn't let them forget his new friends.

'I promise to abide by your decision, Kinleader.' At least for now.

Delvina jogged along the Great Causeway beside Retza, the message cylinder gripped in her hand. The food and clothing outlets were dark and silent, shuttered up with large signs: 'Closed until further notice'. Pale circles from the fading glimmer lights failed to penetrate the long inky shadows in corners and laneways. Only a few toolwuns and workers walked along the broad paths, heads down, furtive glances or eyes to the ground, most heading in the opposite direction toward the outer cribs and crèches. Only the chuckling gurgle of the unseen river, rushing along the deep ravine in the middle of the Causeway, seemed unchanged.

'Where is everyone?'

Retza shrugged. 'In their cribs most like or in the shafts on their shifts. Since the Old Guard attacks and Overseer Havilah declaring half-rations, people aren't so keen to be wandering about in the caverns.'

'At least it's been nine days since the last Old Guard attack and that was half-hearted. Maybe Gilarth has cut off all their access routes, trapped them in the old workings.'

'Maybe.' Retza looked doubtful, his face drawn and fatigue smudged beneath his deep-set eyes. With the thickening stubble on his chin, her twin looked older than when they'd petitioned the Greenstone South Crew to be prentices less than five roster-periods ago.

A rumble came from up ahead, near the commissary supply depot. Delvina's heart thumped a little faster. Another attack? It sounded like many voices, and not happy ones either. Maybe they should turn back. But Overseer Havilah had stressed the importance of bringing the reports from Crib Leadhands and the section Headwuns before the late shift started. Delvina had done the upper levels, Retza the lower ones. She was glad they'd met at the shaft lifts on the way back. The one thing she didn't like about being a messenger was that she and Retza were often separated carrying out their duties.

Delvina moved closer to her twin. 'What is it, do you think?'

'Trouble.' He fingered his lift-bar, his eyes darkening to charcoal-grey.

'We could detour through a side passage.' She didn't want to fight if she didn't have to. The sickening sound and feel of crushed bone beneath her truncheon at the battle of the Sunken Temple still haunted her dreams. The watcher she'd hit had been in a coma for days and was still suffering.

Retza slowed his pace, then shook his head. 'Havilah needs to know what's going down.'

Ahead, outside the commissary's depot, the catcalls and angry shouts increased in volume. The depot doors, flanked by sculptures of Uzza and his father Hezikah, were firmly shut, the windows dark. A hundred crowded around the door and spilled out across most of this side of the divided causeway. By their garb, they were mostly crewless and cesspit workers, lowwuns who lived on the uncertain handouts, occasional jobs and what they could scavenge. Many of the crewless had been pressed as watchers or taken on as prentices to replace those killed in the raids and to staff the double shifts needed for the tunnel project, but not all it seemed. A roar went up through the crowd.

The hair at the back of Delvina's neck prickled. This didn't sound good at all.

'Speak! speak!' Raised fists hammered the air. Faces distorted in the dim blue light.

An angular figure in dark bat-leather jerkin jumped up on the plinth of Uzza's statue and raised his arms wide. A rustle swept through the onlookers like the sound of a bellows on hot metal. Then silence.

'Speak it true, comrade.' Someone at the back of the crowd yelled.

'Speak, speak,' others shouted.

Taking Delvina's arm, Retza eased closer to the edge of the crowd. 'Havilah will need to know what this is about. Tuck your cylinder in your jerkin, though. Don't want anyone guessing we're messengers.'

She nodded, her shoulder tensing as she did as he said. Whatever this was, it wasn't a meet-and-greet celebration. She followed Retza as he skirted around the throng, creeping closer to the front.

The speaker turned slowly, his arm outstretched, palm open. 'It's time to stop the lies. We want the truth.'

The onlookers roared.

'No more lies.'

'The truth, we want the truth.'

The flare of a rag torch lit up the speaker's face as he turned towards them. Narrow, with a half-grown ochre beard, pinkish-grey eyes. Delvina gasped and clutched Retza's arm. 'It's Javot.'

Retza growled. 'What's he up to, then?'

Javot was still speaking '... old guard attacks. And the leadwuns tell the Crystal Heart is fixed. Does it seem fixed to you?'

Another growling roar from the crowd, even louder this time.

'The glimmer lights are fading. Already, the air grows stale, the glimmer trucks go slower than a toolwun walking, soon the potato farms will wither and the glimmer trucks will stop. We are on short rations, less for the crewless and now this fresh order from the new Overseer ...' Javot drew out the title, loading it with scorn. '... who wants to ration the power—to close whole sections or to rotate the power between cribs ...'

'How does he know that? Havilah hasn't even told the leadwuns yet,' Retza whispered.

'It's not right.' Heat flared up Delvina's neck, the worms squirming in her stomach vanished. What was Javot trying to do? Stir up a riot? 'Overseer Havilah and Scrybe Barekia are doing all they can to restore the Glimmer Heart,' she yelled.

Javot stood straighter, his eyes scanning the crowd. 'Who said that? Have we got ourselves a leadwun-lover here?'

The people in front of them twisted around, looking for the interjector, looking for her. Retza gripped her arm, his fierce glare warning her to keep quiet.

Javot smiled like a cave bat swallowing a plump moth. 'And is the Overseer doing all she can?'

The crowd quietened, looked from one to the other, brows furrowed.

'Well, I can tell you. She is not doing all she can. She has vital knowledge of how to restore the Glimmer Heart, and she refuses to act.'

The throng stirred like a swollen torrent.

'No!'

'Shame!'

'What is it? What can she do?'

'Tell us!'

'We'll make her.'

Delvina stilled. Javot couldn't know about the codex, about the cryptic verse—that had been a secret meeting.

Javot lifted his arms high and pulled them down, quietening the onlookers. 'She knows, and she refuses to act out of misplaced compassion, maybe misplaced loyalty.'

'Tell us! Come on, spit it out,' a woman cradling a frail-looking littlewun called from the middle of the crowd.

'Havilah claims there is nothing to worry about, that spilled blood is not needed to save our realm. She's a liar. The old Overseer told us that only our youngwuns' blood could save the Heart of the Mountain. He was a liar and a thief. He was desperate to save his own youngwuns. Only their blood will power the Crystal Heart. '

Someone, an oldwun with a long white beard, stepped onto a storage bin. 'What good is that to us? Uzza escaped with his family to the old tunnels. We are doomed.'

A collective sigh rippled through the throng. Then everyone began talking at once.

Two burly crewless flanking Javot thumped their lift-bars on the ground. 'Let the leadwun speak.'

'Leadwun, my dirty boots,' Retza muttered.

When the crowd quietened, Javot continued. 'But you are wrong, Da-batu. Not all, not all escaped. Havilah has two of Uzza's brats hidden—'

The mob went wild. 'Find them.'

Delvina turned to Retza, her heart thumping. 'We've got to get out of here. We have to tell her.'

Together, they pushed through the dense wall of screaming, fist-waving people, moving closer to one of the foot bridges over the central ravine. They were a few tanis away when someone turned, a crippled woman who'd had a sleeping-patch close to theirs in the Commons.

Her half-crazed eyes cleared. 'I know you two. You used to be crewless.' Her face hardened like old slurry. 'You're her messengers now.'

She reached out her one scrawny arm, grasping hold of Delvina's jerkin. Retza grabbed the woman, pulled her away. More lowwuns were staring, wide eyes slit in suspicion.

The air seemed charged with static, with rage and terror. Hands reached out to grab them.

'Havilah's lackeys.'

'She wants to starve us, maybe we should send her a message.'

'Get them.'

The faces were vicious, even the ones they recognised.

Overhead, there was a rush of noise, a dense coal-black shadow seemed to hover over the crowd, soaking up the faint bluish glow of the glimmer lights overhead and the red gleam of the occasional rag torch, feeding on it, feeding on the fear. Delvina's heart clenched, cold and slow in her chest. Someone seized her plait, pulling her scalp, sharp nails dug into her arm, an elbow dug into her kidneys. Retza was being pulled away as he fumbled to release his lift-bar.

She pushed and shoved and stamped on feet, hit out and slapped aside hands. But there were too many, far too many. Where one fumbled or floundered, another stepped in. She stumbled, clutched the nearest person, her heart racing. If she fell, she'd be helpless beneath the mindless onslaught. She had to get out of here. She'd lost sight of her brother. Panic bubbled up. Catching her breath, she crossed her arms in front of her face. 'Leave me alone. Get away from me.'

A siren sounded, long and loud, pounding in her head, but the hands kept coming, grabbing, the voices battering into her like rocks in a grinder.

'Havilah's lackeys.'

'Get them.'

'We'll show the snitch.'

Strong hands gripped her and she lashed out, scratching and biting. The hands like iron came from behind her, unrelenting, dragging her. Around her the tone of the mob had changed. The sour smell of fear, of uncertainty heightened. Screams sliced the air. Feet running.

The press eased around her, she twisted around. The man, almost as tall as Zadeki, had his arm around her chest, pulling her across the bridge. His face was side on, a straight nose, strong chin. Blood streamed down from above his bronze eyes. The size, the colouring.

'Gilarth.'

What was he doing here? Was he colluding with Javot to overturn Havilah. Had he told Javot about the ikor, about Jesson and Zara?

'Come on girl, let's get you away from here.'

Delvina rooted her feet to the ground. 'Where are you taking me.'

'To safety. I might ask, what are you two troublemakers doing here.'

'We were getting information ...' She stopped, looked about wildly, 'Retza. Where is he.' She turned, charged back towards the melee, looking for his solid build, his jerkin. Gilarth's strong hands caught her again. Held her.

'It's okay lass, Pilay is bringing him out.' Gilarth pointed with his truncheon six tanis to the left, where a watcher stood beside a bloodied and panting Retza, keeping the crowd back, both easing back toward the bridge. Watchers surrounded the edges of the crowd cracking whips to disperse them, detaining a few. Delvina snapped her gaze to the plinth outside the commissary depot, but Javot and his cronies were gone.

Havilah paced up and down the meeting room as Gilarth reported. 'We broke up a mob outside the commissary depot ...'

Putarn and Nebam sat to one side of the room, sorting through a pile of inscribed copper foil, lists of names of those who'd been detained in the riot. Delvina turned her head away, pushing down the smell of fear, the angry yells, the grabbing hands that came flooding back like a blow. Her limbs and face stung with multiple scratches and bruises. Her hands were still shaking.

'Keep still, lass. I can't patch you up if you move like that.' Old Barekia stood in front of her, bandages in her hands, a fist on her hip. Retza sat on another stool, one eye swollen shut, scratches on cheek and arms. At least their hurts were superficial, bruises and scratches not broken bones or internal injuries.

'... riot. Something about the new rationing of the

glimmer lights.' She again caught the thread of Gilarth's report.

'This Javot must be dealt with.' Havilah stopped in front of Gilarth. 'You were meant to discipline him.'

'And I did. I stood him down from the watchers for two rosters on half rations. It didn't deter him from stirring up trouble.'

'Where is he now?'

Gilarth stood straighter. 'My watchers caught him and his leadwuns in an abandoned crib, your Honour. I've confined them under close guard.'

'I know how to deal with the troublemaker.' Putarn stood up and loosened the truncheon tied to his belt, his bearded chin thrust forward. 'Stirring unrest is inexcusable, we can't allow it to spread. I've taken names of those involved.' He gestured to the inscribed copper sheaths scattered across the table.

Havilah ran a hand through her hair. 'True, they should be punished, Secondwun, but just the instigators and not without a decent trial.'

Putarn seemed set to argue, then inclined his head. 'As you wish, your Honour.'

Havilah turned back to Gilarth. 'And Retza and Delvina got caught up in the crowd.'

'Seems so, your Honour.' Gilarth's eyes narrowed as the corner of his mouth twitched. 'Those two have an uncanny knack of being in the wrong place at the wrong time.'

Putarn's mouth twisted. 'Maybe, or maybe not. They were crewless not so long ago, no doubt friends with this Javot—'

Retza barked out a laugh, then clutched his side, wincing. Delvina could see the dark humour of it too, though she found it hard to smile. Javot had been their nemesis before they'd been accepted into the Greenstone South Crew, when Putarn had taken over the role. What was the Secondwun's problem? Surely, after so many rosters they'd proved themselves.

Putarn thrust his head forward. 'Well, what were you doing there?'

Delvina staggered up, brushing aside Barekia's restraining hands. 'We thought the Overseer would like to know what was being said.'

Retza stood beside her, shoulder to shoulder. 'Yeah and somehow, they know the Crystal Heart is fading.'

'Not so hard to work out ...'

'So you say, Secondwun,' Retza continued. 'But Javot knew about the cryptic verse and about Uzza's children. He thinks it means they should be sacrificed.'

Gilarth scowled, his features suddenly forbidding, his big hand tight on the handle of his whip. 'Then someone is a snitch.'

Putarn gave the watcher a level stare. 'I wonder who?' He swung his gaze to include Delvina and her brother.

Havilah put her hand on the Secondwun's shoulder. 'Peace, Putarn,' ... though the worry lines about her tired eyes deepened ... 'this Javot knew about Jesson and Zara, it's not such a long stretch to turn Uzza's policies around like that.'

Putarn shrugged off her hand. 'What if their blood can restore the heart, Matu ...'

Barekia straightened. 'I don't think the crystals work that way, not in the before times, they didn't. It was Hezikah and his son that twisted it into something dark.'

'And if you are wrong, Gamma?' Putarn asked. 'Any progress on that shepherd's ikor riddle?'

'No, but what sort of people would we become to live by sacrificing our youngwuns?'

Silence congealed in the room. Gilarth's face was stony and Putarn's mutinous. Nebam ran his fingers across the lists, his face troubled.

Delvina sat back on the stool. They needed answers. If the Crystal Heart failed and they stayed, they would all die. Not at once, not all of a sudden, but a long lingering death as light and food and air dwindled away in the dark. And there was no escape to the outside.

Delvina caught Retza's eye.

'Do you think he's right?' he mouthed, his face troubled.

She shook her head at him. 'Was it right when it was my blood that was forfeit,' she whispered back. There had to be something they could do. Hadn't it seemed hopeless before Zadeki and Barekia acted?

'The tunnel.' She cleared her throat, making her voice louder so they could hear. 'If the shifts redoubled their efforts on the new tunnels, now the Old Guard's attacks have stopped ...'

Nebam stirred. 'That's our only hope, but we've met difficulties, seams of dense rock that slow our progress, unstable rocks and gravel that make digging dangerous. We're tunnelling blind, not sure where the mountain wall is thick or how high up the mountain the tunnel will come out.' He pulled his scrappy beard. 'It was Uzza and his father that got us into this mess, maybe ...' he stopped, looked down at his worn boots.

'... his progeny should pay,' Putarn finished. 'Two lives for thousands ...'

Barekia threw her thin arms up into the air. 'No, no, no. This madness is seeping into all of us, shadows are swallowing our minds, darkening our hearts.'

'We're trapped in here. If there was another way out.' Nebam rolled the foils, unrolled them, before rolling them again.

'Really, so simple. That's the point, we can't get out.' Putarn thwacked his truncheon against his leg. 'I've better things to waste my time on than riddles. I'd like to see your progress on the tunnels, Nebam, and then I'll check that Javot and his cronies are securely held.' He shot a hard look at Gilarth before heading toward the door. Nebam sent an apologetic half-smile to the Overseer and followed his brother out the room.

Havilah stared at the closed door. 'He watched his father die a hero.' She turned to face them, tears shinning in her eyes. 'Sometimes, it's hard when it seems there is nothing we can do.'

Like Matu and Baba, heroes. Delvina took a deep breath of the stale air. Was there no other way? There had to be. 'Perhaps, Zadeki's people can advise us about the meaning of the codex.'

'Probably they could,' Barekia said. 'But that youngwun hasn't returned and Putarn is right. We have no way to reach him.'

Was there really no way to the outside? 'What about the Cauldron ... '

'The walls rise sheer a thousand tanis. It's impossible, child,' Havilah said.

'Not this crazy talk again, Del,' Retza chimed in.

Delvina raised her voice over the protests, conviction solidifying inside her. 'We should try, at least. I'll go.'

Gilarth cleared his throat and squirmed a little when all eyes focused on him. 'It might be possible ...'

Havilah tilted her head. 'How?'

'At one place on the far wall, there's a scalable rock shaft that cuts into the sheer cliff face for two-thirds of the way to the top. It's hidden behind an outcrop, but I can show it to you. It's difficult and dangerous, but not impossible.'

'You've climbed it?'

'When I was a youngwun looking to escape, yes. Though only part way, to test it. I had hoped to escape with a companion.' He stopped, looked at Havilah, looked down. 'In the end that didn't happen, and I joined the Watchers. Maybe I could go with Prentice Delvina.'

Havilah gave him a half-lidded look and let out a long sigh. 'We can hardly spare an able-bodied toolwun, let alone our Head Watcher.'

Even if Gilarth didn't come with her, he'd given her a possible route to follow. She and Retza had sometimes cleaned the ventilation shafts while crewless, using limbs and body pressed against opposing walls to move upwards. Perhaps, this rock shaft would be like that. It was as though a weight had fallen off Delvina's shoulders. She could do it.

The old Scrybe rubbed her mouth, her eyes crinkled with worry. 'Even if you can climb the Cauldron, Delvina, you will still have to cross the mountains to the Great Forest.'

Delvina stood straighter. 'I'm going to do this.'

'You can't. It's too dangerous.' Retza pulled her around to face him, his face drained of all colour. 'You just can't.'

'I am, I have to. Don't stop me, Retza.'

His chest heaved. He kicked over the stool and grabbed his hair in fists. 'Then I'm coming with you.'

More tension left her. She gripped his calloused hands in her own. 'We can do this together.'

Havilah cleared her throat. 'I'm not sure I'm ready to

lose both of my most dedicated messengers. There's no guarantee Zadeki's kin can help us.'

Delvina turned and cast the new Overseer a beseeching look. 'Do you have any other solutions?'

Havilah ran a thick finger along the edge of her Overseer's insignia, a look of frustration on her face. 'No, though I don't feel comfortable sending two youngwuns into the Outside on a wild chase for answers to an obscure riddle.'

Delvina's chest tightened. She didn't know why, but she knew it was important to find Zadeki's people. If Havilah forbade them to go ... The room seemed hushed, even the sound of breathing muted, just the soft tap, tap of water in a distant tunnel.

'They're strong and resourceful, these youngwuns.' Barekia stood up, cradling the old manual. 'I can't give you the book, Delvina. It is too precious to lose, but I could scribe a copy of the riddle. If nothing be done, it won't matter young or old.'

Havilah's face settled into stone. 'I don't like losing toolwuns on my shift.' Her shoulders slumped. 'But if you are determined ...'

'Yes!' Delvina punched the air, her voice echoing in the large room. 'Thank you, your Honour.'

Retza gave a half-hearted grin. 'Guess we will be leaving, then.'

'Best you give it a day or two, let those bruises heal, at least.' Barekia waggled a bony finger at them. 'And take some keka leaf to help you in the heights.' A small smile spread across her wrinkled face and her eyes brightened. 'If anyone can do it, maybe you two can.'

Retza clung to the sheer cliff face of the Cauldron, his fingers digging into the crevices between the hard rock. His chest craved air and his muscles quivered with the tension, his feet searching for the next foothold. Delvina manoeuvred above him, and a shower of dirt and gravel and grimy snow showered down into his sweaty face. This was crazy. How had he allowed Delvina to talk him into it? But what was he to do? She could be as stubborn as a basalt outcrop sometimes, and he couldn't let her go alone.

The wind thrummed in his tunic and whipped his hair about his face. Its freezing edge penetrated his felt jerkin and burrowed through his ribcage. Jagged grey peaks reared above his head, stabbing into a blue fathomless sky. A sky that squeezed his heart with a fear that even the deepest, dark chasm of the mines couldn't provoke. He refused to look down at the sheer drop to the ledge below. In the deep shadow of the cliff, his back to the open air, he could pretend they were not exposed like uncovered beetle larvae ripe for the picking.

Planning the route up had been hard as they set out in the light of both moons. The first hundred or so tanis of the ascent hadn't been too difficult, with ledges, deep crevices and a slight slope. Gilarth's rock shaft had been punishing but doable, as long as they took it slow. This last section lifted vertically, the rock smooth except for thin cracks barely big enough to jam his thick fingers in and with only small hollows for footholds. Delvina's smaller fingers had found it easier to fit into the non-existent grips. A couple of times, they'd backtracked, but after six hours of climbing they were now near the top.

Truth to tell, it was not the climbing but the deep, bone-numbing realisation that with one slip he would plummet to break his bones on the hard rocks below. Yet, looking up brought little comfort.

The rising sun hinted at its fierce heat as the sky changed from a rich dark-purple to blood-red, sulphur yellow, to the green of tarnished copper. Now the sky was a pale blue, like Zara's accusing eyes and, though still hidden by the precipice in front of them, it made its presence felt, throwing dazzling light off the rockface on the other side of the Cauldron.

He dragged his eyes away from the endless abyss of the sky, away from the bizarre thoughts of tumbling upwards, tumbling away from the firm surface of the earth into that endless blue. Sweat rolled off his forehead into his eyes.

Taking a deep breath of thin air, he dusted his fingers with dirt, one hand at a time, and leaned closer to the cold rock. Gritting his teeth and ignoring the dull ache throbbing in his temples, he forced himself to go on.

Delvina tilted her head towards him. Her pale, speckled face was streaked with dirt, a bluish tinge about the corner of her pale lips. 'I can see a ledge. I think we are almost there.'

'And then what?'

'We find a way down the mountain.'

Retza emitted a frustrated growl as he watched his twin scramble up the cliff face above him. As if climbing down the mountains would be as easy as taking a glimmer lift to the mine shafts. The ancient tunnels under the mountain made a more or less straight route from the Cauldron to the blocked front entrance, some twenty lek distant. One could tramp the distance in fifteen hours if you didn't stop for food breaks. The rough and alien terrain of the mountain skin would make that journey harder. How long would it take to escape these frozen heights?

He stifled the deep trembling in his limbs and pushed himself up to the next hold. His stomach tightened. The only way out was upwards.

Delvina's torso disappeared, then her boots.

Her face appeared over the edge, her pale eyes sparkling. 'Come on, slug.' Her mouth twitched up in a cheeky smile.

Finding a small crevice, he jammed his boot into it, numb hands searching for new grip holes, and he pushed himself up.

Leaning over further, Delvina stretched out a grubby, scratched hand. He grasped it and she heaved until they both lay sprawled and tangled together on an uneven saddle between two peaks. High above them, drifting on the punishing wind, a white-headed eagle hovered. Jagged triangular peaks, cloaked in snow and ice, spread out in a dizzying array from the circular basin of the Cauldron in every direction. Far to the east, in the direction that Zadeki had flown so many days ago, a thin smudge of green lined the horizon.

Retza shivered as the weight of the empty sky pressed down on him, seeming to pin him to the ground. How would they ever reach the distant forests, travelling in the open, without the protection of rock above them?

A cutting wind whistled outside the cave, sending snow flurries swirling around the entrance. The swollen sun, red like a baleful eye, was at last descending behind the jagged peaks. Delvina touched the blisters on her nose with grazed and frozen fingers. Any skin exposed to the blinding sunlight was tight and flaking. She did her best to ignore the pounding head, the grinding ache in her calves and thighs and across her shoulders, the gnawing hunger in her belly.

Each day the burning fiery ball, so much bigger and fiercer than the puny word sun implied, had arced across the sky. A fiery ball that forced them to huddle from its fierce caress in what shelter they could find and travel during the night. The first dark stretches in between the searing light had been lit by the golden moon, but it then it rose later and later each night and the silver moon shrunk to a slim crescent, fleeing the night to become a pale blur against the lapis lazuli of the strange day sky.

The outside world was more frightening and far, far bigger than she had ever imagined. The terrain was like the turbulent surface of an underground river, with peaks and valleys all at odd angles. She and Retza spent hours struggling down the barren slopes and loose screes into deep ravines. Then, after pushing through scraggy grass and bushes or crossing half-frozen streams packed with ice, they'd been forced to climb back over ridges with their treacherous razor-shape edges. The long band of green on the rising horizon grew wider at the end of each night's journey, stretching out into the distance where the sun and moons started their journey. Perhaps the peaks were lower and the air here less thin or cold, but their provisions were already melting away and even more rows of peaks blocked their progress to the distant forests.

Delvina picked up a dried-out branch and placed it on the small fire blazing at the back of the shallow cave. Going back to the entrance, she carefully packed snow into the one iron pot they'd brought with them. It sizzled as she set it on the flat rock placed in the fire. Blowing on her frozen fingers, she stretched them out over the hungry, orange flames.

Her bright idea had seemed not exactly simple but at least doable in the comfort of the meeting room, but Barekia had been right about the punishing heights. Finding their friend in this wilderness seemed impossible.

Her back stiffened. She wasn't going to give up now. Putarn had scoffed at the idea that she and Retza could climb the Cauldron wall, yet they had done it. Pulling out the bird-shaped clay whistle that Zadeki had given her, she blew on it again, hoping that this time it would make a noise. If it did, she couldn't hear it.

Retza stirred beneath his felt cape, then sat up, his messy hair brushing the rough cave roof. Shudders racked his solid body and his face was drawn. His translucent grey eyes met Delvina's for a heartbeat before he looked away and slumped against the rough wall. He didn't scold her for the foolishness of this adventure, though she could see it in his eyes, in the way his blue tinged lips tightened. What if they died here, forever alone, separated from crew and kin? He hadn't wanted to come, had said it was crazy. Her bolstered confidence wavered, acid guilt eating away at the wall of her stomach.

Delvina placed the last of their dried mushroom and slithers of smoked cave fish into Retza's mug and poured some of the steaming melt water over it. Saliva flooded her mouth at the tantalising smell. She offered the mug to her twin, giving him most of her own share in mute apology. If there a source of food in the barren wilderness, neither she nor Retza had been able to find it. He gulped down the broth and then thrust the cup into her hands, half full.

She shook her head. 'It's yours.'

'We both need to be strong.'

Once she swallowed the delicious mouthful, she stood and gathered her gear. Retza groaned and did the same. Ducking her head, she stepped out into the soft grey light that seemed to linger as the sun dipped down behind the jagged skyline. Retza stumped in front of her and took the lead and the full force of the buffeting wind for this shift. She clutched the copy of the instructions the old Scrybe had written out for her. A soft sorrow welled up and brought tears to her eyes. It was hopeless, beyond crazy. Perhaps they should go back.

She hitched her pack higher on her shoulders and opened her mouth to say the words, then snapped it shut again. Havilah, Barekia and all the cavern people were depending on her and Retza to find answers. The above-grounder, Zadeki hadn't given up. Not when they'd found him with a broken wing in the Cauldron, nor when he had been the prisoner of the Greenstone South Crew, not even when it looked like he would be sacrificed to the Dark Ones along with her and the others, supposedly to bring the Mountain's Heart back to life. And because he hadn't given up hope, they had been able to defeat Uzza and drive him from the main caverns. Perhaps, Zadeki's Maker would guide her as it had guided him. Would the guardian of the above-grounders be interested in the people of the deep mountain caverns?

Around them, the light faded from the sky. Pink bled into deep amethyst-purple and reflected off the snow heaped in the hollows. The glow-worm stars winked at her in their swirls and roped patterns, as though they were on the verge of speaking, of whispering their secrets. She quickened her pace.

A deep, icy silence settled around them. They pushed on, through the comforting darkness of the night. Heaviness settled into every pore and muscle. Golden Alumi sank towards the western skyline while the shrinking silver moon rose in the east, splashing a silver glow on the distant horizon. Retza stopped so suddenly, her head butted the back of his shoulder.

'What is it?'

He pointed to a broad band of blue-tinged white blocking their route. 'It looks like a frozen river.'

'Are rivers that broad or lumpy, even frozen ones? It's got to be at least two hundred tanis wide.'

'Who knows in this upside-down world.'

She nodded and put the clay bird whistle to her chafed, cracking lips and blew, as much out of habit as hope. Then pulling her cap further down her head, she followed her brother to the strange expanse glowing in Argenti's pale light.

The cold from the river of ice seeped through the leather soles of Delvina's boots and chafed her feet. Head hunched down to the buffeting wind, she placed one blistered foot in front of another, her eyes gritty with exhaustion. Light was beginning to creep above the mountains, the sky's deep aubergine bleaching to grey, the silver glow of the crescent moon leeched out by the coming dawn.

'We should find somewhere to stop and wait out the sun.'

Delvina started at the hoarse sound of her brother's voice. His teeth chattered with the cold. The sparse stubble on his chin and upper lip were rimmed with ice.

He wrapped his arms around his sturdy chest. Such things didn't happen in their world, where the temperature was even, and the rocks grew warmer the deeper one went.

Cold seeped into her bones like despair. If she lay down now, she might never get up. 'We've got to find a way down soon or we're not going to make it.'

Retza blinked, his pale lashes like stubby gold wire in the first rays of the sun. His head jerked a nod of sorts. 'We have some time before the sun begins to sear our skin.'

He didn't add that they'd come too far to turn back, that they needed to find food after days of trudging through this beautiful, perilous, bleak landscape. He didn't have to say it.

They walked side by side, shoulder to shoulder, squinting against the radiance of the rising sun. The profound silence surrounded them, hardly dinted by the crunch of ice under their feet, the rustle of their ripped clothes and the whine of the wind. Her ears longed for the march of many boots, the ringing of metal picks on rock, of voices singing the rhythms of the work, the dripping and running sounds of water, even the buzz of an insect or the chitter of cave bats.

Almost as though she had conjured it, her ears caught a soft musical murmur, hauntingly familiar though with a strange timbre. The sound of a stream came from far beneath them, somehow higher pitched, more threadbare, more exposed than the chuckling torrent that ran through the deep ravine in the middle of the Great Causeway. The sound was soothing, like a lullaby Matu used to sing—

Retza stopped dead 'Watch out,' he yelled. his voice pitched high and urgent.

Before she could stop, Delvina's front foot stepped out into a chasm of open air.

Her back foot caught on the churned-up ice on the edge, before slipping and sliding down. She twisted and grabbed for a hold, anything. Her heart pounded like a toolwun's hammer on molten metal. Her fingers grabbed the edge, scrabbling for purchase on the slick knife-sharp surface. Her legs slammed into the ice-cliff and she jerked to a stop.

She took a shuddering breath and looked up into Retza's alarmed, sun-pealed face. He knelt perilously close to the edge, his fingers gripping her jerkin, his eyes wide. She hung against a white blue-shadowed ice wall. Small rivulets of melt water ran down its cracked face and the ground, or rather the pool, lay five hundred tanis beneath her boots.

'By the pit, Del. I can't keep holding you while you take in the sights.' Sweat beaded on Retza's forehead. His corded neck and face reddened with the strain.

Terror slammed into her. She jammed the toes of her boots into the splintered wall and gripped what handholds she could.

'Pu...' She swallowed and forced the words out. 'Pull me up.'

She pushed against the ice. He pulled, the jerkin lifting up to her ears. Breathing hard, Retza heaved and she slithered over onto the frozen river.

She collapsed on the wet, slippery surface, the sun hot on the back of her neck. Her left ankle, her knees and the tips of her fingers throbbed, but she was alive. Her heart and breathing slowed to normal.

Retza thumped her shoulder. 'Don't scare me like that.' His eyes shone and he turned his head away and sniffed.

'Sorry.' She sat up and peered out over the chasm.

Less than a pace in front of her, the ice ended abruptly. Far below, at the base of the frozen ice-fall, a pool reflected the sapphire of the sky. A braided river ran down the centre of a deep valley, the water casting a dazzling light like molten silver. Above them, a bird drifted in lazy circles.

Delvina breathed in sharply, her chest swelling and a new burst of energy coursing through her limbs. 'If we follow the river, it should lead to the forest, like Barekia told us.'

'We just have to get down there.'

'We climbed the Cauldron. We can manage this, but let's rest first.' It wasn't going to be easy, but maybe they could reach the forest and find their friend, Zadeki. She only hoped he had the answers they needed. Whatever happened, it was better to die out here, searching for a solution, than huddled beneath the fading glimmer lights and stale air below, knowing they hadn't tried.

Zadeki glided above the forest canopy, the wind ruffling his flight feathers. He effortlessly kept in formation with the rest of the scout group. They'd only one sighting of the wild tribes people hunting peccary further up river. Low grey clouds veiled the afternoon sun and white streamers drifted up from the ravines in the thickly wooded slopes. The highland mist forests were not as hot as the Great Forest, where most of the kin-groups were harvesting the sava roots and seasonal fruits. Pickings were slimmer here but still enough to feed their group. The wide land was bountiful in all its manifestations—grasslands, deserts, mountains and dense forests—for those who knew the song-lines. The dangers were there too, the wild tribes with their arrows and poison darts, the fierce animals—crocodiles, jaguar, pythons—but nothing his people couldn't handle. The Vaane were a different matter.

On his left, the group leader, Ehu, whistled the return-to-base signal. Keeping in formation, Zadeki banked and headed back toward the lone white rock spearing out of the dense patchwork of greens like a bony finger. It was one of the Kin's many meeting places and the closest to where he'd come out of the mountains. Damatu had called together the elders and most this side of the mountains had responded to the call. Getting them to agree on strong action would be a slow process.

At the base of Fang Rock, the shelters clustered on a slight rise. Zadeki circled, angling his flight feathers as he banked. In the centre of the clearing, the designated cooks were building up the fires for tonight's meal, while the foragers brought their finds. On a ledge further up the rock, the Kinleader stood with a group of elders. Josenif and Benjim stood a little apart, closer to the edge.

Ehu and the others landed in the clearing, transforming into their human forms. Zadeki gave a downward sweep of his wings, swooped over his companions' head and used the warm eddies off the rockface to propel him up to the ledge. As he skimmed the ground, feathers and wing bones shrunk, legs and torso lengthened and he hit the ground running. Arms outstretched, he slowed his momentum before he crashed into his brothers.

Josenif caught him by the shoulders. 'Whoa there, scamp.'

Zadeki wrapped his arms around Josenif, practically

lifting him from the ground, then slapped Benjim's shoulder. He couldn't stop a huge grin spreading across his face.

'You're back. Did you find the earthbiters? Did you make contact?'

'Peace, son of Korak. Your brothers are making their report now,' the Kinleader's face was severe, though a smile lurked in her green eyes.

'In other words, son of my brother's son, sit down and shut up,' Aunt Bikan said, her dark eyes snapping.

Dipping his head in acknowledgement, Zadeki sat to one side, grateful he hadn't been sent away.

'Go on, oldest son of my son's son,' Da-Matu said.

Josenif touched his chest. 'After a couple days flying, we found this Cauldron, as Zadeki described it, near the Misty Peaks. We searched the sides of the steep crater walls for an entrance to the underground realm.'

'It is a large area roughly circular and about ten lek across, filled with pine and brush and a small tarn,' Benjim added. 'But no entrance.'

'Yes, and covered with fresh snowfall so all trails were cold, even to jaguar senses.'

What? That sounded like the Cauldron, but how had they not found the tunnel. Zadeki jumped up. 'There's this big hole in the side of the mountain, on the south side. You'd have to be blind to miss it.'

Benjim glared back at him. 'What are you saying younger brother?' Then he laughed, his dark eyes crinkling. 'We did find the tunnel once we'd circled the Cauldron a couple of times. It has been sealed off by large rocks so that it blended into the cliff face.'

Josenif shook his head. 'We tried to shift the boulders, but some were too big, and we couldn't make a way in.'

'We hollered and called out and waited some days, to see if earthbiters would come out, but no one did. So, we thought it best to come back and report.'

Zadeki fought against the sinking feeling in his gut. 'There was no rockfall when I went through it. Are you sure you found the right crater?'

Benjim's eyes darkened. 'What, you think we're stupid, little brother?'

Josenif placed a hand on Benjim's shoulder. He fetched out an object tucked in his sarum and held it out on his palm. 'I found several of these planted outside the barrier.' He showed it to the Kinleader, then the elders before offering it to Zadeki.

He held a stick carved with a spiral of monsters.

Aunt Bikan stood up and wrapped her tari tighter around her sparse figure. 'A warning stick. It is clear the Darane do not want our aid.'

Zadeki chewed his lower lip. It didn't make any sense. How had the rocks got there? Havilah was not like Uzza or Hezikah to close off the entrance. Surely this meant his friends were in more danger not less. 'Can't we still help?'

The Kinleader shook her head. 'My daughter is right. We do not interfere in the internal affairs of other people unbidden. May the Maker preserve them.'

'But ...' While Zadeki could feel the Kinleader's compassion, her voice was firm. He only hoped his friends were not in dire need. 'Can't you at least keep watching?'

The Kinleader hesitated, then nodded. 'Very well, we can spare a few pathfinders to patrol the mountains, but beyond a full cycle of Golden Alumi, we cannot stay.'

Retza took the lead. Despite the cold and the slick ice, the climb down seemed easy after the Cauldron. It took them most of the night. At the bottom, a craggy jumble of ice pushed up against a rim of heaped gravel and scree. Water seeped and pooled and then ran in a foam-edged stream.

They filled their water bottles and kept going as the sky lightened and blushed in pinks and reds. The line of the valley led them downwards and mostly to the east, the high mountain peaks were behind them. The valley, steeped in deeper shadow than the heights with the sun still behind the ridges, felt less exposed and safer. At least while the sun was low in the sky.

Retza's stomach growled. Each day, the gnawing pains became harder to ignore.

'Perhaps there are fish in the stream.' Delvina's voice echoed his thoughts.

'Not that I've seen. Nor snails either.' Retza chewed his bottom lip. The milky, grey water criss-crossed over loose gravel and rock rubble, joining and splitting off in fast, shallow streams.

It was hard to imagine what kind of creatures lived in this exposed world anyway. He'd seen no mushrooms or algae. Insects and creepie crawlies seemed scarce in the punishing cold winds and were hardly worth the bite anyway. The rare birds flew too high or fast to catch. Living on the surface, so unprotected was still hard to comprehend. There was something unnerving about the ever-changing march of clouds across the sky, the sudden change of temperatures, the way rain or snow would fall on their heads without warning.

The flat valley floor widened out as they tramped, the ridges on both sides further away and not as steep. The vegetation on the eastern slope was sparser, with what looked like thick, grey, branching columns covered in spines. Squat and stubby trees crowded on the western slopes of the valley. It could provide shelter as they slept during the day, but they needed to eat.

'We could forage for food in the bushes.' Picking up a handful of small rocks, he threw one and watched it ricochet off the boulders and tree trunks.

The stone tumbled to a stop, the sound echoing through the valley. To the left a sudden flurry of movement caught his gaze. A group of grey shadows dashed out and bounded towards a clump of dusty bushes and spiky plants. He ran after them, letting another rock fly at the closest creature.

'Quick, Delvina, head it off.'

Acting in step with each other, as they had so often done in the Commons, they cornered one of the creatures against the cliff face. It wasn't as big as he first thought, but big enough. Grey fur, a pointy face with small rounded ears, small front legs and a long muscular tail. He had no name for it except dinner.

Delvina let out a soft sigh. 'It looks so sweet.'

'By the pit, Del, we've got to eat.'

'I know, but I don't have to like killing it. Are you sure it's not Zadeki's Kin?'

Retza hesitated—trust Delvina to think of that—and then shook his head. 'Don't worry, it'll fly away or at least speak if it is.' Or at least, he hoped so.

The creature's ears swivelled, its nose twitching. It leaned forward, power gathering in its hindquarters. Before Retza could move, Delvina dived on top of it, grabbing it around the body. Retza bashed its head with the stone. The creature jerked, laid still, blood seeping into its fur and dripping to the ground.

Delvina's arms began to shake. A tear glittered on her

grimy cheek. She let go of the creature. It flopped against the rocks. 'It's bigger than a cave-rat or even a bat. It's not going to fit in the cooking pot.'

Retza dropped the rock and wiped his smeared hands on a bush. 'We could roast it.'

They made a fire beneath an overhang in the side of the valley, Retza gutted and skinned the animal while Delvina fetched water from the stream for drinking and washing. As the fire died down, he raked glowing coals into a heap with a branch and threw on the carcass.

Retza sat back against a large boulder and took off his boots and wiggled his toes. He was used to tramping long distances in the tunnels, but the chilled water, wet boots and sudden temperature changes had made a mess of his feet. Red, painful blisters shot sharp pains up his leg.

Delvina sat beside him, huddling close. She took the clay whistle out of her tunic.

'You've been doing that since we left. It's not even making a sound.'

Ignoring him, she put her chafed lips to the opening and blew hard, puffing out her cheeks. Nothing happened, not a wheeze or a whimper. Perhaps there was a special knack to it.

She blew again. 'He said to use this, if ever we wanted to speak to him.'

He grunted, not bothering to reply.

The sweet aroma of roasting ground-bat mingled with wood smoke and the strange tangy smell of the straggly leaves. His stomach growled more insistent than before. Not waiting until it was fully cooked, he pulled it from the fire. Together they ate their fill, before crawling under the bushes to sleep.

Delvina pulled apart the remains of another of those small furry creatures they'd caught and roasted at dawn. Food wasn't plentiful, but they'd managed to scrounge enough to dull the gnawing hunger over the last few days. Each day the line of malachite green on the horizon had grown thicker, and shaggier. Each day, it became more obvious that the forests stretched from north to south and toward the sunrise, as endless as the sky. Rivers—some red, some silver, some a muddy green—wound through the patchwork of greens like veins of metal. Not just one, hundreds of them. The scale of this above-ground land stole the breath from her bellows. She put the whistle to her lips and gave a half-hearted puff.

Retza stood up with a grunt. He threw the gnawed bones on the cooling fire and looked at her from below his pale eyebrows. 'Even if we've reach the forest, how will we find Zadeki? We could look a lifetime and still not find him.'

Delvina lowered her head. Tearing the last shred of pink meat from the bone, she gulped it against the tightness in her throat. She looked back over the serried rows of mountains they had spent days traversing.

'Listen, Del, we could collect enough food for the journey home.' He ran his hand over his grimy face. 'If Javot is stirring up riots or the glimmer lights keep fading, Havilah will need every strong hand she has.'

Had they really come so far, survived so much for nothing, for a handful of fool's gold? The sensible thing was to turn back. 'But that's why we have to try, Retza.' She would keep going even if he turned back, though she didn't know how she'd do it without him.

'Another shift then, but at some point, we'll have to

accept we've failed.' He stood up and kicked dirt and gravel over the sullen coals of their fire. 'Let's get going then.' His voice was gruff, his eyes avoiding hers.

Throwing the bones into the bushes, she grabbed her pack and headed away from the sinking sun. Argenti had long fled behind the western horizon. The glowing half-circle of the golden moon leered at her high up in the domed sky. Rivulets of water in the deepening stream chuckled and sang. All around them, small jewel-like birds trilled in the sparse bushes. Bright flowers sprung from bizarre growths on the trunks and branches. It was as though she was caught in a dream.

A long keening whistle echoed in the valley. A large bird with grey feathered body and white head and a wide wingspan floated high above them.

'Retza, look, doesn't that look like Zadeki's bird shape?'

Her twin shrugged. 'Yeah, seen them often. Doesn't mean it's him.'

Another bird swooped in from the side, its hooked beak gaping as it let out the high-pitched call.

Both birds dove down towards them. Delvina brought her arm up, shielding her eyes, her heart in rapid beat.

A double thump, the sound of slithering stones and a shadow fell over her. She lowered her arm a fraction and blinked. Two people, a man and a woman, towered over her, their silvery-white skin rosy in the late afternoon light. They wore simple clothing wrapped around the waist and a loose length of cloth looped over the shoulder, just like Zadeki did, and the one with wider shoulders had the same wavy black hair and coal-black eyes as their friend. Suddenly she felt light, like a bubble rising in a hot spring.

'Are you Zadeki's Kin,' she blurted.

Retza lowered the arm clutching a rock, his eyes rounded.

One of the above-grounders lifted her hands. 'We are, children of the mountain. Why did you call us?'

Had they heard the silent whistle? 'We need to talk to Zadeki. Is he here?'

The man took a step forward and tilted his head. 'He is some days' walk to the east at Fang Rock. You can speak to us.'

Could she trust these tall above-grounders? Standing shoulder to shoulder with Retza, Delvina thrust out her jaw. 'We don't know you. We will only speak to Zadeki.'

Zadeki splayed his toes, his feet gripping the rough bark of the swaying branch, one hand on the branch above. He reached up and twisted the ripe fruit free. A gentle breeze ruffled his hair, evaporating the heat on his skin. The pinnate leaves rustled their secrets around him. Once the baskets were full and his foraging group returned to the camp at Fang Rock, he would swim in the river with his cousins and other kin. Zadeki inhaled the sweet aroma before throwing the fruit into the basket on the ground below. It hit the rim, teetered a minute, before falling on the mound of its fellows.

'Hey, watch out, that almost hit me,' Ehu called up.

'The rest of the fruit of this tree is not yet ready,' Zadeki called back down. 'Let's move to the next one.' He wiped the soft sheen of sweat from his brow and stretched his cramped muscles, his toes gripping the tree branch. Through the gap in the leaves, he could see snowy peaks, like fingernails poking up beyond the green-clad mountains. What was happening to his friends in the deep caverns under the mountains? Had Havilah sealed the Cauldron door against intrusion—from him and his kin? Or was the reason more sinister?

A young skinny girl in a short white tari came running along the narrow trail below, her dark hair flying out behind her.

'Zadeki, Zadeki,' she called, her bright eyes scanning the trees.

It was Ehu's little sister, Tiah. From the crown of the giant seiba tree, a bunch of red and green parrots took sudden flight, screeching their displeasure.

She drew closer and she rushed up to her brother. 'Ehu, have you seen Zadeki?'

'He's up there ...'

Zadeki swung down the branches until they ran out and then slid down the trunk, his feet breaking his fall. He stretched out his arms to regain his balance and grinned.

'What is it Tiah?'

Tiah tilted her head to look up at him, her dark-green eyes big and round in a slender face. 'The Kinleader wishes to see you.'

His heart began to race. 'Did Da-Matu say why?'

Tiah wound a lock of hair around her finger. 'No, but, Josenif and Umbria have brought strangers back with them from the mountains.'

'The sons of Tamrak?' asked Ehu.

'No, these two are short and stubby. Their eyes, hair and skin are as pale as woodworms that haven't been exposed to the sun. They say they will only talk to you.'

Zadeki's eyes rounded as excitement bubbled up inside his chest. The mountains. This had to be about the earthbiters. Surely the Darane wouldn't have broken through the front gate just yet. But why else ...

'Thank you,' he called to Tiah as he raced towards Fang Rock.

'Hey, wait, who's going to carry the basket?' Ehu called after him.

Zadeki didn't have time to answer.

Delvina stayed close to Retza as the tall above-grounders led them along a small stream and into an opening in the dense forest.

At the edges of the space, several flimsy structures of wood and leaves balanced on tall poles in a semi-circle. White smoke filtered through the leaves, its pungent smell tickling her nose, along with the aroma of unfamiliar food and the deep, rich scents of mud and leaves. Maybe fifty people, tall adults and children of various sizes, were scattered around the clearing or working beside the stream. They stopped their activities and stared as she and Retza followed their guides toward the biggest shelter. Behind the clearing, the ground swelled into a hill and then rose sharply, a spur of white granite thrusting up into the grey sky like a broken tooth.

After two days of travel, it was good to be no longer hemmed in by the rustling, creaking trees that crowded so close to the pathways. The trees were better than the open sky, making travel by daytime possible, but not by much. Especially when she'd realised that many of the strange noises were made by the weird creatures that inhabited this realm, some bigger than they were. And even under the fragile roof of the tree's foliage, water could drop out of the sky at any moment.

Retza pointed past the shelters to the hill. 'Is that where your caverns are?'

The woman, Umbria, gave a musical laugh. 'We don't live below the ground entombed in cold hard rock like your people, Retza.'

'And these are all your crew?' Delvina tried to keep her disappointment from colouring her voice. Somehow, she'd thought Zadeki's people would be skilled and wise or at least more numerous than this, not living like a bunch of crewless beneath flimsy shelters. Where were the stone houses, the halls, the supply depots? There was no sign of great cities or crystal technology or even of guards. How would these simple folk be able to help them?

'This is but part of a family group, daughter of the deeps. Many of our kin are at the sava harvest in the Great Forest.' Umbria's tone was slow and patient, as though speaking to youngwuns.

'Truth be told, our folk are spread across the great land from the boundless sea in the west, the forests and the highlands of the mountains to the green bosom of the mother forest.' The man who looked like Zadeki's twin, Josenif, spoke, an indulgent smile on his face. 'We are many, though not as many as the people of the Lonely Isles.'

An older woman with oval face and sharp eyes placed the basket she was holding on a mat and stepped toward them. 'Nor as many as the fast multiplying children of the younger peoples, filling up the land as fast as a river in flood.'

Delvina's stomach tightened at the woman's acerbic tone. She glanced at Retza, met his frowning stare. Who were these younger peoples and why did they attract this woman's scorn? He looked as much out of his depth as she felt.

'As you say, sister of my father's father,' Josenif nodded. 'Will the Kinleader speak to our guests now?'

'Indeed. She would see these children of the stone.'

Delvina drew herself taller, though her head didn't even reach the shoulders of the shortest adult present. 'We wish to speak to Zadeki.'

Beside her, Retza planted his boots on the damp earth and nodded. 'Where is he?'

The older woman clicked her tongue. Taking a deep breath, she swept a hand toward the onlookers gathering around them. 'Here is the Kinleader now, earthbiters. She will tell you.'

The throng parted and a woman walked towards them. Though short for the Kin, her posture was powerful and poised. Her flowing silver-streaked hair reached to behind her knees.

'Zadeki is coming, for I have already sent for him.' She spoke with a melodious voice.

The Kinleader wore no insignia of authority that Delvina could see. Her garb was simple like the rest of the forest dwellers and her feet bare, yet the others parted with deference, letting her pass through their midst.

The woman stopped a pace away from them. Short as she looked beside her own people, Delvina tilted her head to meet her gaze. Except for laugh lines, her silvery-white face was smooth. Her grey-green eyes held the echo of long ages.

'Zadeki tells me that Hezikah is dead and his son, Uzza, deposed.'

'This is true.' Retza fingered his lift-bar. 'You know our people? Who are you?'

'Once, Hezikah's father and I played together. Once ...' she stopped, a sad smile played at her pale pink lips.

'Well that is a song for another time. I am Telsima and I am honoured to be Kinleader of these people.'

'Barekia says it's over two hundred years since Hezikah closed the Glittering Realms, she was a littlewun at the time and now she is ancient. You do not look as old as she.'

Delvina could only agree with the sceptical tone in Retza's voice. This woman looked no older than Overseer Havilah, surely less than one hundred, yet to have played with the old Overseer's Da-baba as a child—that would make her impossibly old, as many as four hundred years.

'Our people, the Forest Folk, or should I say, my mother's people, live longer than most, though I can see that it is hard for you to believe. Not to worry. As you won't speak to us, do at least take some refreshments while we wait for Korak's impetuous son to join us and allay your suspicions.'

Delvina glanced at the rickety structures with misgiving. Would they hold the weight of so many people? 'We ate not so long ago.'

Telsima tipped back her head and laughed, a joyous, free sound. 'Do not worry, I will not make you climb for your supper. Though sleeping on the ground even in the Mist Forests has its own hazards.' She turned and beckoned the people behind her. 'Bring a mat, food and drink for our guests for it is such a long time since Darian's people have shared food with us.'

The clearing erupted into activity as one brought a mat made of thin, flat sticks, an intricate and colourful scene of the mountains woven into it. Another approached with a finely woven basket filled with clear water. Josenif and Umbria scooped up the water, washing face and hands, and drying them on small cloths offered by a young woman. Meanwhile, a troop of tall, slender children in flowing white clothes spread out bowls of food and containers of drink on the mat.

'Would you like to wash, honoured guests?' A young boy almost as tall as Delvina stood at her elbow, dark eyes wide.

Delvina chewed her lip. Would it give offense to refuse? She stepped forward and copied Josenif's actions, and sat down on the mat where indicated. She glanced up at Retza and with a muted growl, he followed her actions.

The Kinleader settled in front of them, her movements as supple as a youngwun's. She cupped her hands against her breast. 'For the Maker's provision, we are thankful,' then she spread out silvery arms, 'All are welcome. Eat.'

The small but plenteous bowls of food were full of a strange collection of presumably edible things. The forest dwellers ate with their fingers, often dipping them in small bowls of water to rinse them. Though Delvina's stomach grumbled with hunger at the savoury fragrance, her fingers hovered over each bowl offered to her. Some looked like cooked leaves or roots, others held rolled up balls of white stuff sprinkled with seeds. Only when she saw the snails in a green tinted broth and a bowl of fried mushrooms, did the tension release in her shoulders. At last, something she understood in this strange land.

Even as she savoured the salty, earthy flavours, a commotion arose from one side of the clearing. She looked up, saw a group of large red and green birds fly from the canopy and circle the clearing. A bush swayed near a track and then Zadeki's fleet figure came racing towards where she sat with Retza.

Zadeki slowed to a walking pace and approached. He

placed two hands over his breastbone and inclined his head. 'Kinleader.'

The strange old woman rose to her feet, the others following. 'Son of Korak, it seems the children of the mountain seek your help.'

Zadeki nodded then spun around and swept Delvina up in a huge hug, a grin splitting his face. Delvina half laughed and half coughed, her ribs squeezed and breath hard to catch, but suddenly sure everything would be alright. He had saved them before, he would save them again.

He set her down, turned and wrapped his arms around Retza, who struggled to escape. 'We gotta breathe, you know,' he rumbled.

Zadeki released him and grinned wider, his dark eyes alight. 'It's good to see you two.'

He turned to others sitting beside Telsima. 'Baba. Aunt Bikan'

'It's good to see you being so prompt, youngest son,' the older man said drily.

'Yes, Baba.' Zadeki put on a more serious face, though the corners of his mouth twitched up. Josenif jumped up and clapped him on the shoulder. 'We found your earthbiters some hundred lek south-west of the Cauldron.'

Zadeki tilted his head. 'How did you get out? Has Havilah opened the front gate?'

Retza massaged his ribs. 'No, all who try are killed by the hidden traps. Nebam is digging another tunnel, but it's slow and there are barriers to overcome.'

'Then how?'

Delvina touched Zadeki's arm. 'We climbed the walls of the Cauldron and came across the mountains.'

A soft murmur ran through the Forest Folk standing

at a polite distance. Some had returned to their duties, the children resumed their play but others, it seemed, watched them with interest.

'That seems an unlikely story. How would you survive.' The woman called Bikan turned to Josenif. 'And didn't you say the entrance was blocked.'

Delvina's smile faded. She bit her lip and shook her head. 'The entrance to the Cauldron wasn't blocked when we left over two rosters ago.' How did this happen and why? Tears gathered in the corner of her eyes. Were they too late to save their people?

'Why would you attempt the climb, Delvina? What's wrong?'

'The Crystal Heart is dying. It has taken us so long to find you, perhaps already it is dead.'

Retza cleared his throat. 'Delvina thinks you can help us.'

Bikan folded her arms. 'Zadeki can barely keep himself out of trouble.'

Delvina wondered at the dismissive tone. 'His courage and insight saved us from Uzza's madness and the Dark Ones.'

Zadeki flushed, moving from one foot to the other. 'Oh, but I ... we just distracted the guards while Scrybe Barekia fixed the Crystal Heart. If she doesn't know how to fix it, how could I help?'

Delvina took a deep breath. 'Barekia found a manual for the Glimmer Heart. There is a bit that might help, but we are not sure of the meaning. Perhaps you could tell us.' She pulled out the cylinder from her pack, unrolled it and put the metal foil, etched with the Scrybe's carefully copied words, into Zadeki's hands.

Zadeki blinked and peered at the spidery scrawl on the scrap of thin copper. He read the words so all could hear. 'To the chosen shepherd attune, to red heart's beat vibrating, and in true seed's crimson ikor replenished.'

He was touched by Delvina's trust in his abilities, but this was beyond his ken and he could only disappoint her. Taking a deep breath, he bowed his head and handed it to the Kinleader. 'Da-matu, perhaps you can help us?'

Her wise grey-green eyes held his. 'I see you have not told us everything of your escapade, young Zadeki.' She glanced at the writing and handed it to Bikan. 'You are keeper of the scrolls, my daughter.'

Aunt Bikan's eyes lit up. She bent her head and studied the words. 'It is hard to be sure of the meaning without the full context.'

Delvina gripped her hands together, her wide, snub-nosed face creased with worry. 'Please, our people may already be dying. Can you help? What is a shepherd, what is the seed and what is ikor?

'A shepherd is a keeper of animals, I think.' Zadeki said, not sure if it were so.

'Tamrak's children herd yarma and the Vaane have sheep and goats on the Lonely Isles, but the Darane are not keepers of animals,' one of the men said.

'A shepherd is a leader, a guide who tends the welfare of those in their keep. The Kings and Queens of the old world were often called shepherds.' The Kinleader tapped her long ivory fingers on her upper lip. 'It is they who developed the crystal power, and it destroyed them in the end.'

'The Sea Dragon King's crystal technicians on the Lonely Isle would know,' Baba said.

A younger man stood forward from the watching group. 'It is many day's flight to the star followers' harbour at Redhaven, even further by foot or hoof. Besides, the Vaane's white ships are overdue by many cycles of the Golden Moon. It would be long before such advice could be sought.'

By then it might be too late. 'Someone could fly across the silver sea,' Zadeki said.

'That is not so simple, my son. Few still know the albatross or dolphin forms or the secret to finding the Isles in the vastness of the towering waves.'

Aunt Bikan folded her arms. 'As you say, son of my brother's son, and when our messenger arrived in Silantis, the Vaane would leave us cooling our heels for days before their high and mighty would agree to see us. Even if they'd wish to deal with the mountain people after Hezikah's rebellion against them.'

'Still, the Sea-Dragon throne is in disarray, with no clear heir to choose from. The Grand Technician may wish to re-establish relations with the Overseer under the mountain. The followers of the stars are greedy for the earth's riches,' Baba countered.

Delvina and Retza's round eyes seemed almost to pop as they looked from one speaker to another. Zadeki could feel their amazement and confusion like a fog around them. Their pale faces blistered from the sun, their realm with its tunnels and mines was so different from his. They must wonder at this talk of ships and waves and distances and kings. The wind rustled in the tall trees and long shadows stretched further across the clearing as the sun slipped down the sky. Zadeki wrapped his sarum around him, as the sweat from running chilled on his skin.

Delvina touched his arm, her pale eyes wide with trust. 'Is this King a leader like the Overseer or,' she looked at Da-Matu, 'the Kinleader?'

Da-matu smiled and took her hand. 'Yes and no, daughter of earth. Have your people forgotten their own songs? The first Dragon King laid claim to all these lands. He installed Darian as Overseer of the King's mines. Darian's people worked hard to dig the tunnels and excavate the ore and often for scant reward. Then, Overseer Hezikah, Darian's descendant, broke with the King and shut off the Glittering Realms from the outside world.'

Zadeki looked at the Kinleader with new eyes. How did she know so much about the Mountain people? Still, she had lived many of the sun's song cycles and would have travelled to the Glittering Realms before Hezikah shut the gates.

'I had not heard this before. Nor has Barekia mentioned it.' Delvina rubbed her chin. 'Then, do the Forest Folk look after the trees for this King, as my people look after the mines.'

A soft rustle swept through the gathered Kin and Zadeki grinned. As though the Kin would work for the Sea Dragon King. Even Da-matu smothered a smile.

'No, our history is not so simple as that, but that is a song for another day,' she said.

Retza wet his lips. 'If the King across the sea is the shepherd, would he help us?'

A golden ray of sunlight pieced through the foliage, lighting up the tip of Fang Rock. An idea bubbled up, like trapped air in water. Zadeki slapped his thigh, making the twins jump.

He grinned. 'Maybe it isn't the King. If the Overseers lead your people, assigning work to the Crews and controlling the Crystal Heart, perhaps they are the shepherds?'

Da-Matu nodded. 'This could be, for the glimmer crystals under the mountain were bonded to the Overseer.'

The talk of kings, ships, oceans and animal shepherds seemed as foreign as sun and sky, but Delvina understood about Overseers. Feeling light with hope, she gripped Retza's arm and he smiled back at her.

'Overseer Havilah is the shepherd? If she finds this ikor, she can revive the Crystal Heart?' That must be it. She knew Zadeki and his people could help them.

The Kinleader held up a hand. 'If she is a descendant of Darian or indeed of Hezikah and Uzza. The bond is tied to Darian's bloodline and renewed in each generation.'

'I doubt she is, though.' Retza said in a low, gruff voice.

Delvina's shoulders slumped and elation shrivelled a little. 'So Uzza is the shepherd.' How would they get him to help them, even if he still lived. 'What of the 'seed'?'

The brusque woman, Bikan, waved a hand. 'That part is simple. The seed would mean his offspring. And ikor is an ancient word for blood.'

'The Overseer's heir could be the seed?' Retza asked.

'So the words would mean ...' Delvina swallowed hard. 'To the chosen Overseer attune, to red heart's beat vibrating, and in true heir's crimson blood replenished.'

Retza moved closer, his rapid breath loud in her ear. 'Then Javot was right, the Heart crystals requires their due, the ikor of the Overseer's children.'

Delvina twisted around, her blood congealed like cooling lead, and met Retza's gaze. His face was as appalled as she felt. 'Surely not.' But what else could it mean? Her heartbeat thundered in her ears as she held Retza tight.

His dark eyes troubled, Zadeki moved closer to them. He gave a tremulous smile. 'There has to be another meaning.'

Zadeki's Baba stepped up behind him. 'As power-hungry the wielders of the crystals are, not even the Sea Dragon King required child sacrifice to fuel his power.'

Kinleader Telsima nodded. 'Such deeds would feed the dark shadows in this world, but the glimmer-heart crystals do not work that way.'

'Then what can it mean, Kinleader?' asked Zadeki.

'This I cannot tell you. We are not soul-bound to crystals. Our gift does not require it. Our song-lines are of forest, field and mountain under the sun.'

'Then you cannot help us?' Delvina sunk to the ground, burying her face in her hands.

Had they crossed the mountains for this? Though, whether it helped or not, Havilah needed to know the cruel meaning of the riddle.

Retza gripped her shoulder. 'Sister, all is not lost.' He turned to the tall forest people. 'If your people could bring food and materials. Even wood for fuel. Perhaps our leaders can complete the tunnels or break through the door before the Heart fails.'

Bikan clicked her tongue. 'We are not Tamrak's children or the Vaane to store up food in stone houses. The wide lands provide all we need in their times and seasons.'

'Can nothing be done?' Zadeki jumped up, throwing his hands in the air.

'Calm down, youngling.' Telsima's voice had the strength of folded steel. 'We can gather enough food to supply the immediate need of our cousins beneath the mountains ... and trust the future to the Maker. You do not object to that, eldest daughter?'

Bikan opened her mouth, closed it and shook her head. 'They ask for our aid. We should do what we can. Though how will you carry it? Who will you send?'

Telsima nodded. 'Korak take what food we can spare. Choose who you wish to help with the journey. I will send more later. Better take this young scamp along with you.'

Korak smiled. 'As you say, Kinleader.'

Zadeki blinked. 'Me?'

Kinleader raised her dark eyebrows, 'Since you started this rescue mission, it behoves you to finish it.' She looked thoughtful. 'And maybe it's time I revisited the mines, too.'

A broad smile spread across Zadeki's face. He turned to throw his arms around Delvina and Retza. 'It's going to be okay.'

Delvina certainly hoped so. If only they could bring the food back in time. 'They could already be in dire condition.'

Retza banged his fist on his thigh. 'And even if we leave this moment, it will be twice as long before we return.'

Zadeki looked to his father. 'We could fly.'

The older man nodded.

'You will go ahead?' Delvina's shoulders sagged. It would be days before she and Retza could return, to find out if the mission had been in time. Would it be enough?

Korak squeezed Zadeki's shoulder. He turned and smiled at her, his eyes kind. 'Don't worry, daughter of the mountain. We can carry you.'

Eyes squeezed shut, Retza clutched the shaggy coat of the great flying beast, a koraktil or so Korak had named it, his knees clinging to its wide girth, Delvina clutching his jerkin. The wind rushed and buffeted against his face, lifting the beast's dark mane, ruffling his tawny crest and the pitch-black wing feathers. In the west, the molten red ball was sinking behind the far horizon. Below them, the long line of snow-capped peaks, spread out like a crumpled cloak. While he and Delvina would have preferred to travel by the moons' light, the sun's heat was necessary to provide the wind currents according to Korak. Zadeki and Josenif accompanied the three koraktils in eagle form.

'We're almost there.' Delvina yelled in his ear. 'Are you okay?'

'Scared out of my wits.' Retza looked over his shoulder and shouted into the thunder of the wind. 'And I thought scaling the heights was terrifying.'

'Hang on,' The koraktil's voice vibrated in Retza's chest, somehow it was still recognisable as Zadeki's Baba.

Korak tilted and plummeted towards the landscape of rock and ice below. Retza felt himself slipping forwards, Delvina's weight and the force of the load pressing against him. He dug his fingers into the thick fur and closed his eyes, as the ground rushed towards him with dizzying speed. The tugging forces of the freezing wind dropped abruptly and moments later, Korak's broad back lurched.

Prising his eyes open, Retza let out a relieved breath, as the familiar walls of the Cauldron towered around them from all sides. His heartbeat slowly returned to something close to normal, and he rubbed his moist hands on his breeches. It was hard to believe that a journey that had taken them so long, had been completed in a couple of terrifying, mind-paralysing hours.

'You can open your eyes and dismount now, Retza, Delvina,' Zadeki's amused voice came behind them as he circled on outstretched wings.

Retza took a deep breath and slipped off the broad back of the strange creature. Not unlike a gigantic bat or bird, though it had a long-toothed snout, four stout legs, a black furred body, broad feathered wings, and a long scaly tail. Korak folded his wings and shook out his mane. Twisting his long neck, he blinked at Retza. 'Can you remove the burdens?'

Zadeki banked and came in fast. Even before he hit the ground, his bird shape shivered and stretched into his human form. He grabbed the rope harness and unbuckled the straps. Overcoming, the shakiness in his legs, Retza rushed up to help, Delvina joining in. Together they eased the large baskets packed with food and essentials on either side to the ground.

With a powerful downdraft of mighty wings, the large black shape of another koraktil swooped over them and landed on some level ground a few paces away. Telsima sat on its back, her silver streaked hair streaming in the wind. Her cheeks were flushed and eyes bright as two full moons.

'I'm starving. I could eat tomorrow,' Zadeki said, rubbing his stomach.

Relieved of his burdens, their koraktil reared up on its strong hind legs and shrunk into the tall, lanky form of Korak. 'Not as ravenous as me, youngest son.' He turned to Retza and Delvina. 'Let's eat, then we can move some rocks from the entrance and get these provisions to your people.'

Telsima leapt off the back of the second koraktil. 'Yes,

though so a few of us should go first, to scout out what state the people are in.'

Retza's stomach tensed. He could only hope the help and supplies they brought would be enough.

Delvina swallowed against the tightness in her throat as she hurried along the tunnels toward the Causeway. Retza, Zadeki, Josenif and Telsima jogged behind her.

The glimmer lights were like pale after-images, barely lighting up the empty space. Where normally hundreds of toolwuns would push and shove their way through the crowds, nothing moved except for the rats and the bats. A rank, stale smell clogged her nose and the air was stuffy and flat. Not even the vents were working properly. The supply outlets in the Great Causeway had shutters smashed, goods strewn across the concourse, food ransacked. Dark, inky shadows congregated in the corners and laneways. The glimmer lights so weak, they seemed to make the darkness stronger.

Too late, too late, too late.

Bile rose in her throat. What if Overseer Uzza had been right all along, and she had saved her own life only to doom her people to eternal darkness?

Retza gripped her arm. 'Perhaps they are in the Grand Cavern.'

'By the Maker's favour,' Zadeki said, his face slack with shock.

They rushed along the Causeway. Avoiding the glimmer-lifts, which would surely no longer work with the failing Heart, they took the stairs and the passageway to the Grand Cavern.

The inner entrance stood open, the metal doors bent and battered. Dark mounds scattered about revealed bruised and bloody faces and crooked limbs, some with damp patches beneath them. Delvina shuddered. Were these Old Guard or their own?

Retza knelt beside one of the bodies, touching the pallid skin. 'Still warm.'

'Then, all may not be lost.' Telsima's silvery voice echoed off the walls.

Tears choked Delvina's throat. She averted her eyes, edging past the bodies to the door.

The Grand Cavern was a confusion of shadows. Red, flickering light seeped from tunnels, competing with the ghostly glimmer lights. The great bronze doors still stood closed against the outer tunnels. She frowned. Who had attacked the watchers? Had the Old Guard tunnelled through rather than batter down the door? Distant shouting came from the tunnels and closer to hand, a hushed rustling in the far corner of the huge space.

A dark figure started up from the side and flicked on a glimmer torch, flooding her face with light. 'Who goes there?'

Blinded, Delvina shielded her eyes with her arm. 'Where is Overseer Havilah?'

'Rebels, seize them.'

Two figures charged towards them out of the shadows, truncheons raised. Delvina ducked then hit out at the nearest one. Beside her, a blur of movement and Zadeki and the two shapeshifters stretched out into jaguar form, bounding past her, pouncing and swiping. The torch fell with a clatter to the stone floor and soon the guards were pinned down under their great paws. Retza and Delvina fastened the three captives, tying them together.

'Over here,' a hoarse voice called out.

Grabbing the torch, Retza shone it towards the back of the cavernous hall. A large group of people sat huddled in the corner, the whites of their eyes gleaming in the cold blue light of the torch.

Delvina pulled tight the last knot, picked up a fallen mallet, and stood. The three jaguars bounded off in different directions, prowling and sniffing the corners of the room. Many of the group shrank back, some crying out as a jaguar neared them.

'It's okay,' she shouted as she rushed toward them. 'They've come to help us.'

Among the frightened group she could see the battered faces of Gilarth and Nebam and Havilah.

'Delvina. Retza. You brought help?' The Overseer's hair fell about her face in mattered tangles, her voice weak with relief.

Delvina knelt and cut the knots around Havilah's wrists. 'As soon as we could, your Honour.'

Havilah gripped Delvina's hands. 'You both are as brave as your parents. Is one of the jaguars Zadeki?'

'Yes, and two of his Kin, Joesnif and the Kinleader, Telsima. What happened? Did the Old Guard return?'

Beside her, Retza began loosening Nebam's bonds, then Gilarth's.

'Not that.' Havilah pushed herself up from the wall, then collapsed with a groan. 'The glimmer lights were fading. People were afraid. Many whispered we should have given the sacrifice to the Dark Ones or sacrificed Uzza's youngwuns as Javot had told them. I refused to allow it. He escaped somehow and incited the crewless and more than half the watchers to attack.'

'He is in the Heart room with Uzza's youngwuns even now.' Gilarth's voice was hoarse, one eye bruised and swollen shut, his jerkin crusted with dark blood. 'It may already be too late.'

Havilah grabbed Delvina's wrist. 'Did you find the meaning of the riddle?'

Delvina glanced at Retza. He nodded and continued to release the other captives.

'Shepherd may refer to the old Overseer, the "true seed" to his children and ikor means blood.' She sucked in the foul air, her heart pounding like ore-crushers.

Nebam looked troubled. 'Javot was right? Is this the only way the Crystal Heart can be restored?'

Delvina sat back on her heels, the mallet in one hand. 'The Kinleader thought it must have another meaning or the manual could be misleading.'

A jaguar padded up beside them and spoke with Telsima's voice. 'Even if it is, should you build your safety on the blood of innocents? If the Crystal Heart dies, then find another way to survive.'

Nebam rubbed his wrists and grimaced. 'The privileged son of the old Overseer is no innocent. His father and his father's father before him robbed us, living in luxury while we struggled and half-starved. Worse, they killed our youngwuns and we accepted it.'

Gilarth growled deep in his throat. 'Havilah, you promised their safety.' He lurched to his feet and staggered, clutching his side. Some of the other released watchers grabbed him, but he shrugged off their hold.

One of the jaguars, Zadeki she thought, growled. His tail lashed back and forth, his lips curled back in a snarl, exposing huge canines. 'Would you punish the children for the crimes of their fathers? Havilah, you can't agree to this.'

Havilah held up a hand. 'There is no time for discussion. Besides they have Barekia and Putarn.' She looked at Retza and then Delvina. 'Go! Go now and save them all if you can.'

The jaguar with a silver muzzle reared up on hind legs, her form changing into the Kinleader. 'Yes, go, before it's too late. I will see this place is secured and join you soon.'

'Let's go.' Zadeki spun around on his haunches and bounded toward the tunnel door that led to the Heart Room. The other jaguar, Josenif, a whisker behind him.

'Come on, Retza.' Delvina grabbed her mallet and raced after them.

Heavy footsteps followed behind. A quick glance showed Danel, Gilarth and Nebam and at least five other released watchers and toolwuns crowded behind her and Retza, jostling together as they entered the tunnel. Some of the tension eased from her shoulders. They had backup, but by Zadeki's Maker, she hoped they were not too late.

Zadeki felt the cold stone flow beneath his paws. He bounded down the passageway, pushed on by urgency. Though he'd met them mere Alume ago and even though they might have taken his life, he would do all he could to save Delvina and Retza's kin. At the end of the long tunnel, the door to the Heart Room stood ajar, still damaged from when he had broken down the door with Retza and Delvina a couple cycles of Golden Alumi ago.

Two stocky earthbiters in worn clothing stood before the broken door with truncheons and lift-bars. Their pale eyes widened and the sharp scent of fear added an edge to the mix of stale food, grime and sweat. Zadeki wrinkled his nose but did not falter, keeping pace with Josenif's long bounds. Surprise and momentum would be to their advantage.

'We've got trouble,' one of the earthbiters hollered. Lifting their weapons, they charged towards them. Zadeki put his head down and together he and Josenif bowled them over, the earthbiters' boots skidding on the slick stone, arms and legs a tangle.

'Keep going. We'll secure these two,' Danel yelled from behind them.

Zadeki leapt through the door into the high-roofed room, more a large cavern than crafted space. A handful of earthbiters milled around near the middle, scrambling to pick up weapons. The warm, earthy presence of his underground friends crowded behind him.

In the centre of the room, the giant Crystal Heart pulsed with a weak, greenish light as though life was oozing from it. Three people were tied fast to the panel at its base. Barekia's white hair straggled from her messy bun, flopping over her bruised face. A girl about Delvina's age and a small boy were roped beside the old Scrybe. These must be the younglings Delvina spoke of. Relief flooded through Zadeki. They were still alive.

A couple of earthbiters rushed towards the door, weapons raised, mouths wide in wordless yells. More formed up behind them. Heat rushed through Zadeki. Power curled in his muscles, pooled in his paws. Opening his mouth, he roared, the vibration singing through his throat and chest. The earthbiters faltered.

Josenif growled beside him, 'You have the speed Zadeki, save the children. We'll hold off this riff-raff.'

Zadeki flicked his tail and nodded. 'Retza, Delvina, follow me.'

Changing his angle, he stretched his limbs and bounded toward the Crystal Heart. A fighter came at him from the side, but staggered as a hammer thrown by one of Havilah's watchers hit the man's chest. A cheer came from behind him. In three bounds, he was at the Crystal Heart. Pulling to a stop, he placed a sheathed paw on Barekia. She was in a worse state than he'd first thought.

'Free the youngwuns first,' she mumbled through bruised lips.

That made sense. It was the younglings this black-hearted Javot wanted, yet the old Scrybe didn't look well. He hooked the boy's bounds with a claw, careful not to rip tender skin. The youngling screamed pulling away from him.

'Keep still! I'm here to help,' he growled, trying to make his jaguar voice reassuring. Thwacks, grunts and yells came from behind him, the smell of blood and the thud of running boots.

The girl, her chin quivering, kicked out with her feet. 'Leave my brother alone, you great beast.'

There was no time to explain. He ignored the girl's blows and sliced through the ropes holding the boy.

Suddenly, Retza was beside him. 'Peace, this is our friend. We're here to save you.' He whipped out a knife and cut the girl's bounds.

The girl grabbed the youngling, pulling him against her chest. Her face was wild, blue eyes staring at Zadeki as though he was a monster. Retza helped her up. 'Come, Zara. We need to get you out of here.'

Zadeki glanced back at the melee in front of the door. Three earthbiters were running towards them, only paces away. He turned ready to free Barekia, but Delvina crouched beside the old woman, slicing at the ropes with her knife, the pink tip of her tongue between her pale lips. She looked up at him. 'I can carry her. Get Javot.'

Zadeki spun round and faced the advancing

earthbiters. Which one was the leader? His tail lashed from side to side, his hackles raised. He could smell their fear and sense the darkness in them. It inflamed him. A growl rumbled deep from within his chest. Two of the earthbiters slowed and faltered, waves of terror emanating from them. The narrow-faced one with a pushed-down nose kept advancing, a long sharpened pole held out in front of him.

Zadeki feinted to the side, then, spun, reached out, wrapped his great paws around the pole, wrenching it from the man's hands. It clanged and clattered to the floor and rolled away.

The man reached for his knife hilt in his belt. Zadeki leapt, grabbing him in a tight hug, rolling on the floor. He felt a rib crack beneath his paws.

The man screamed. 'Help me.'

'Javot, he's too big,' a quavering voice responded.

'We didn't volunteer for this,' the other one said.

He must have Javot pinned down beneath him. 'I have your leader,' Zadeki roared.

Rich, metallic blood dribbled from the man's lips. He struggled and pushed, his tender neck exposed. Zadeki licked his lips and pulled himself back from the strong urge of jaguar thoughts. Keeping his captive pinned down, he scanned the room.

Retza and the younglings had reached the door. Gilarth, Danel and an earthbiter he didn't recognise were rounding up and securing injured combatants. Josenif was herding the two that had deserted Javot, their knees shaking so much they could hardly walk. Beside him, Delvina supported Barekia as she hobbled to the group at the door.

The battle was all but won, but something was out of place, his fur ruffled with a sense of hidden danger. The room was full of a medley of warm-blooded scents, both fresh and stale. He curled his lip to catch a musty odour, one he should know. He growled.

Beneath him, Javot squirmed. 'Spare me.'

'I'll take him off your paws.' The earthbiter in watcher's bat-leather said. 'We've got the lot.' An uncertain smile flickered on her drained face. 'You aren't going to eat him?'

'Don't tempt me,' Zadeki backed off and swivelled his ears. The slither of boot leather on metal, the puff of sour breath.

The flash of black flickered in the corner of his vision.

'Delvina, watch out. Zadeki.' Retza yelled a warning.

Zadeki spun around. A thickset form dropped down from the pipes. Delvina stopped, stood in front of Barekia and put her hand on the mallet hooked into her belt. Barekia straightened, her grey eyes wide, 'Putarn?'

Yes, that was it. What was the son of Havilah doing here. How had he managed to escape his captors?

Knocking Barekia to the floor, Putarn reached out and grabbed Delvina. Rage suffused his face. He twisted Delvina's arm behind her back.

The Secondwun was hurting his friends. Zadeki gathered his remaining strength in his hind legs, wriggling his hips as he lined up his prey, when something heavy hit his side, pushed him off balance. Despite the sudden pain, he turned and swiped at a white-faced Javot, lift-bar in hand. The woman watcher who'd offered to secure Javot, stood behind him, a smirk on her face. She'd tricked him. Further back, Retza and Gilarth were running towards them. Dodging Javot's lift-bar, Zadeki grabbed him by the chest and pulled the man down. The bar clattered to the floor.

Zadeki spun around, ready to leap at Putarn, when the woman launched herself on his back, sticking her fingers in his eyes and tangling him in her cloak. Javot and two other watchers piled on top him. Pinned down and entangled, he roared with frustration. Had he saved mad Uzza's children, only for his friend to lose her life?

Cold, like a deluge of icy water, drenched Retza. His sister was in danger. They'd always been together, always protected each other, no matter what. Retza gripped his lift-bar and roared. He ran toward the Secondwun, ready to smash him to the ground.

Delvina was struggling in Putarn's grip. She hit out at him and stamped on his toes. The Secondwun punched her head, her eyes glazing. Free from the flurry of blows, Putarn whipped out a long obsidian knife and held it to her neck.

'Be still, girl, or I'll slice your gullet.'

Retza ran faster. Just a few more strides and he'd take the traitor down.

Putarn glared and snarled. 'Don't come any closer.' He looked around wildly. 'Not one of you move.' Drops of bright blood welled from Delvina's neck.

Zadeki roared from behind in his jaguar's voice. 'Retza, he'll kill her.'

Retza stopped mid-step, his muscles quivering to keep his balance. Purpose flashed in Putarn's amethyst-hard eyes and thrust out chin. Beads of blood dribbled down Delvina's neck and pooled in the hollow in front of her collar bone. A flick of the wrist and ...

Retza's stomach clenched. A wave of nausea swept through him. 'If you harm my sister, I'll cut you into tiny pieces and feed you to the cave-crays in the cesspits.'

Putarn barked a laugh. 'If you even twitch, slug, your sister is dead meat.'

Something brushed his shoulder and he jumped. Havilah stood beside him, her hand on his shoulder, her broad face drained of all colour. 'Let me speak to him.'

The Kinleader stood further back, blending in the shadows. He hadn't heard her arrive, too focused on his sister.

Havilah's fingers dug into Retza's shoulder as though she was drawing strength from him. She cleared her throat. 'Putarn, my son, why are you doing this? Why are you working with this crewless Javot?'

Putarn's mouth twisted as though he'd tasted something bitter. 'Maybe mad Uzza got it wrong or hoped he could spare his own children by sacrificing our youngwuns. But the manual makes it clear what is required.' He shot the Overseer a hard look. 'You're a coward, Matu. You just don't have the courage to act. I'm not going to let you stand by as our realm sinks into darkness.'

'I told you, boy.' Barekia grimaced as she propped herself up on her elbow. 'Pouring blood over the Crystal Heart, whether it be Uzza's own or bat ikor, isn't going to make a pinch of difference.'

'So you say, Gamma, but you know different. You should have told us how it is done so the Glimmer Heart can be restored.'

'What you are doing will accomplish nothing.' She collapsed to the floor, cradling her arm. Her breathing was laboured. She was old and Javot and his thugs had clearly not treated her kindly in their search for information.

'Putarn, this is not the way.' Havilah held out her arms, her mauve eyes pleading.

He snarled. 'Sometimes the few die to protect the many. Isn't that what you said when my father was taken. You just stood there. Your inaction killed him as surely as if you held a knife to his neck, and now you blame me for taking action. You can't hold me back this time.'

Havilah's shoulders slumped, a hand cradling her neck.

'It wasn't like that. What you are doing is different.' Barekia's voice faded as she spoke.

'Putarn, brother, this is madness. Put the knife down, and let me help Gamma.' Nebam took a step closer.

Putarn's hand jerked, the drip of blood swelled to a trickle. Delvina's eyes widened and Retza's heart slammed against his ribs, taking his breath.

He grabbed Nebam's arm and screamed. 'Don't move.'

It would only take a second for the sharp, sacrificial knife to slice through skin, muscle and blood vessels, to steal his sister's life. The air in the cavern seemed to have been sucked out the ventilation shafts.

'Enough talk. The boy should be enough. Bring him to me,' Putarn ground out between clenched teeth. 'Or I will kill this troublemaker.'

Jesson sobbed and pushed his face into Zara's skirts. She wrapped her arms around him. Her pale pink lips parted as though she would speak, but no words came.

Josenif's backed away a fraction.

'Don't move,' Putarn screamed, drops of sweat beading on his forehead. 'I know what you're up to. Give me Uzza's littlewun, and when the deed is done and the Glimmer lights are restored, I'll let this prentice go free.' He swept his gaze over the watchers. 'And then, when I'm vindicated, maybe we need some real leadership.' His wild eyes looked past Retza, to Nebam. 'Brother, you know that I'm right. You could be my Secondwun. Release my men and tie up these fools.'

Nebam glanced at the old Scrybe slumped on the floor. His face hardened, and he shook his head. 'Matu is right, this isn't the way to do things.'

Putarn scowled. 'Fool, you will regret your choice.' He turned, pulling Delvina with him. 'Who stands with me? Bring the youngwun to me.'

For a moment, no one moved. Then Javot got off from Zadeki. Clutching his side, he stumbled toward Jesson. A couple of Javot's men pushed themselves up from the ground, nursing their injuries. Zadeki was still weighed down by the other thugs, his black roseate fur bristling, his tail lashing.

Who could help his sister? He struggled for breath, his jaw aching.

Putarn's face relaxed into a smile. 'Come, Prentice Retza. You're a sensible fellow. Is your sister's life worth this pampered son of Uzza? Help Javot and you'll have a place in the new order.'

'No! Please!' Zara backed away, clutching Jesson tighter. 'He's just a littlewun. He hasn't harmed anyone.'

Retza gripped his lift-bar harder. The boy's life or his sister's. He sucked in a jagged breath, his eyes meeting Delvina's.

The corner of her lips quivered, as though she was trying to smile. She licked her lips. 'It wouldn't be right and, anyway, you can't trust him,' she said, her bright eyes trained on him. 'Take him out. I'm willing to ...'

Putarn slammed his head against hers. 'Shut up, slug.'

Retza's hands shook, tears blurring his eyes. He wanted to pound Putarn into the rock for hurting

Delvina. She was all that mattered. And what if he and Javot were right and the youngwun's blood would save the realm, as well as his sister. Uzza wouldn't hesitate.

'Isn't it the Dark Ones that need appeasing?' Zara's voice cut across the cavern, holding a challenge.

Retza turned and met her fiery blue gaze, and she lifted her chin though it wobbled.

Putarn spat on the ground. 'So said your baba, girl, the revered Overseer and his lackey priest, but the manuals say otherwise. It's the crystals that need ikor, not the Sunken Temple's pit.'

Two spots of red flushed on Zara's cheeks. 'Then take me instead. I am Uzza's daughter. If the bloodline of the Overseer is required, then why not mine?'

Jesson looked up, horror mirrored in his wide pupils. 'No!'

'No! Lady Zara. Let it be me.' Gilarth clenched his fists, speaking for the first time.

'Gilarth, you know that cannot be. You are not of Uzza's bloodline.' Zara's eyes softened. 'Look after Jesson.' Soft hands trembling, she prised the littlewun from her flowing skirt and pushed him toward Havilah, who grabbed the struggling child, holding him tight.

Zara took a slow step forward, her hands held out in front of her. 'Take me.'

Relief rushed through Retza, and shame at the same time. She may be Uzza's daughter, but she was brave, and it didn't seem right that she should die.

For the first time Putarn looked uncertain. He glanced at Javot.

The former crewless scratched his beard and then thrust out his lower lip.

'She's too old, she's not a youngwun anymore.'

'I'm not much older than these twins. Does your precious manual stipulate the age of your victim? '

Javot scowled. 'You said I could have her if I did your bidding and stirred up trouble for you, said your words for you.'

'You were the leak, Putarn. You told Javot about the codex,' Delvina's voice was soft and hard at the same time.

It had been Putarn all this time. Blaming him and Delvina or Gilarth for the leaks. Retza tightened his grip of the lift-bar. 'You are the traitor.'

Nebam growled. 'What the prentices say is true. You betrayed us, brother.'

'Do you think I was going to stand by and let our realm slide down the refuse shuts to be buried in shadows? Now do as I say.' Putarn turned to Javot. 'There be other girls. You can have your pick when I'm Overseer. Bind that one's hands behind her back and bring her to me.'

Zara lifted her wrists to Javot.

Retza hands were slick on the lift-bar. The thought of Zara' death left him hollow. She was Uzza's daughter and willing to give her life up for Delvina's as well as her brother's. She was their adversary, yet she shamed him.

The cold volcanic blade, felt like a fire brand across Delvina's neck. One hairy arm gripped tight against her, crushing her ribs, restricting her breathing. His legs trapped her own, pinning hers together. Which was perhaps as well, as they felt as liquid as slurry.

While Putarn's attention has been diverted by the girl, Zadeki pushed up and shrugged off the rebel watchers holding him down. His dark eyes were fixed on her, his muscles rippling beneath his skin. Yet, the second he leapt, Putarn would end her life. The Secondwun was hungry for blood—if not hers, Jesson's or Zara's, and when would that blood lust stop? She could struggle, and he'd kill her. Zadeki's Maker help her, she needed to think. She didn't want to die, but she didn't want Zara or Jesson to die either.

'What had Zara said, 'bloodline.' She licked her dry lips. 'Scrybe Barekia is right. You're reading the manual wrong. It doesn't say sacrifice.'

'If you don't shut up, I'll slice your neck, girl.'

Delvina laughed, shaky and more like a sob. 'If you kill me, you've lost your leverage and Zadeki, Retza and Gilarth will make crushed ore of you in a heartbeat.'

Javot wound a rope around Zara's outstretched hands, tying tight knots. Havilah held back a sobbing Jesson. Nebam hovered behind his mother, his face slack with shock. He hadn't joined his brother, which was a blessing. Only two of Havilah's watchers had turned, disarming and tying up their companions. Josenif, like Zadeki had edged a fraction closer, though still too far to help. And, hadn't she seen the Kinleader come in with Havilah. Perhaps, she had imagined it. She sucked in the stale air. There must be another way.

'The Kinleader said the crystals don't work that way. They are soul-bound.' Her forehead crinkled in concentration.

Putarn squeezed her chest tighter. 'Shut up.' His foul breath blasted her face, turning her stomach.

Zara tilted her head, her copper hair a nimbus around her pale face. 'The Heart is soul-bound.'

'Right, trying to talk your way out of it now.' Javot

pushed Zara forward. 'Guess you would be too much trouble, anyways.'

Retza took a deep shuddering breath. 'What if she's right? You would have blood of an innocent on your hands.'

'Innocent?' Putarn hawked and spat on the ground. 'Besides, what if she's wrong? How many innocents die then? Would you have the whole realm on your conscience—all the toolwuns, littlewuns, oldwuns? Javot, bring the wench. I haven't endless patience.'

'This isn't the only way, Putarn.' Havilah held out an arm palm up.

'Enough talking. Bring the girl.' Sweat rolled down Putarn's face.

Javot grabbed Zara's bound arms and pulled her along, his narrow eyes bright. 'Come on then, little jewel.'

This wasn't how it should end. There was only one thing she could do. Delvina sent a mute apology to Retza. His eyes rounded, horror seeping in, and he mouthed, 'No'. She dropped her head and bit hard on Putarn's meaty hand, stamping down on his foot.

'You, mouldy she-bat.'

She felt the stinging slice of the knife, a roaring in her ears. The rush of wind and darkness surrounded her. Someone was screaming but it wasn't her. Putarn's arms dropped away and she slumped to the ground. There was shouting. Suddenly, Retza's arms were around her, he was pressing his fingers against her neck to stem the flow of warm blood. Black spots congregated at the edge of her vision. She took a ragged breath, felt for her neck. It was slippery with blood, but somehow she was still alive.

The light trembled. She glanced up. A large dark shape fluttered around Putarn. He was screaming, his hands thrashing and grabbing at the black thing, silver streaks along its torso and on its muzzle. She blinked. It was a bat, bigger than any she ever seen, swooping and diving, its black wings in constant motion.

She sank to the floor. Retza stripped off his jerkin, wadded it up and pressed it against the wound. His fingers trembled and he gripped her hand. 'I thought he'd killed you.'

Danel and one of the others grabbed Javot, while Gilarth, Zadeki and Josenif converged on Putarn.

Zadeki pounced on him first, wrapping his jaguar paws around Putarn's legs, bringing him crashing to the stone floor. The bat flew free, swooped across the roof of the cavern.

Josenif pounced on Putarn's chest. Gilarth stood over them, panting, truncheon clutched in his strong hands.

He scratched his messy hair sticking out from under his helmet. 'Maybe, I should bash the brains out of this one.'

'No, tie him up. He and Javot will stand trial for what they've done.' Havilah's voice held the frigid ice of the mountain passes.

'And so he should,' Josenif growled. He sat back on his haunches, and so did Zadeki.

Putarn's face and arms streamed with blood from long curved scratches. Gilarth hauled the former Secondwun up.

Putarn's face contorted. 'You fools, you have doomed us.'

'Maybe not.' The bat swooped down, its legs expanding, its wings shrinking, it's face rounding, the fur sinking into silvery-white skin, flowing out on top in long black and silver streaked locks. The Kinleader stood beside the Crystal Heart. She examined a hand and sighed. 'Though I think I've broken a fingernail.'

Zadeki held a cold compress to his side, where Javot had whacked him. Nothing broken, just bruising. His injuries were not serious unlike poor Barekia. Retza shifted beside him, clenching his hands together, his pale grey eyes fixed on his sister. Brave Delvina looked small, like a youngling's wooden doll, lying on the pallet as the Kinleader peeled off the stiff cloth covering her wound. Delvina's pale face was shadowed with pain, her eyes hazy with the keka leaf Da-matu had given her.

Across the cavern, Havilah and Nebam hovered over Barekia, examining the old one's injuries. Zara sat close by, her face dazed and Jesson asleep in her arms. The debris of the struggle lay about them. Gilarth and Josenif had taken Putarn, Javot and the other rebels to a holding cell.

'Keep still child.' The Kinleader put the cloth, stiff with dried blood, to one side and washed the seeping wound on Delvina's neck. 'You took a great risk. Any deeper and Putarn's knife would have done irreparable damage.'

Using a heated steel needle, she threaded the skin edges shut. Delvina gripped the edges of the palette she lay on. She moistened her lips. 'Would the Secondwun have stopped at one death. Once you were all disarmed and bound, he would have had you in his power.'

'In truth, there are not many bindings that can hold us.' Telsima tied off the knot and stood back, examining the wound.

And this was true, especially if one knew many forms.

Zadeki bit his lip. He knew only two. 'But, Da-Matu, why did you not attack earlier.'

From across the room, Havilah nodded. 'Yes, we are grateful for your ploy, but we could have done with help sooner.'

Telsima placed a clean pad of stagmoss on Delvina's wound and used a long cloth to fasten it. 'In truth, I thought the exchange between Delvina and Zara would provide a distraction, but this impetuous daughter of the mountain, forced my hand—or wings, rather. There that should do it.' She washed her hands in a basin, glancing over to where Havilah and Nebam knelt beside Barekia. 'How is the Scrybe?'

'Not good. How Putarn could do this to his Gamma, I don't know.' Havilah heaved a sigh. 'She has taken a severe beating and broken bones in her fall. I've splinted her arm. It is the bruising on her head that worries me most. Perhaps sleep and time with help.'

'I will get my people to bring healing herbs.' The Kinleader stood up and walked over to them. She placed her hands on the old Scyrbe's face and chest. Tipping back her head, she sang high and sweet. The words brought with them the sound of the wind in the trees, a memory of the living green of the forest. After a few moments, Barekia's laboured breathing eased. 'Her will to live is strong.' Telsima turned and looked Havilah in the eye. 'What is it, daughter of Elad? You are troubled.'

Havilah looked up startled. 'How do you know? I haven't been called that in a long time.'

'You have the look of your father, daughter of the mountain.'

Havilah ran a hand over her dishevelled grey hair. 'I

must thank you, Kinleader. Though the Glimmer Heart still sickens, the supplies you have brought will hold us for a while.'

'For now, yes. We can gather more to bring to you, but I fear it may not be enough. In part because we are not a people who stockpile food. The Land is generous and provides our needs without such bindings to place. And then, only three of our people know the koraktil form. There is a limit to how often they could fly, how much they can carry.'

Zadeki clenched his hand. Another form for him to acquire and one hard to do, as the koraktils lived far to the south. Josenif was right, he had much to learn and no matter how he helped his new friends, their situation only seemed to worsen. What they really needed was to restore the Glimmer Heart.

Havilah nodded. 'I understand. We must redouble our efforts on the tunnel so that necessary supplies can be brought in. Unfortunately, many have been injured or disabled with my son's foolishness, and I fear for the farms. Even if we could make our way out of the Cauldron and climb down to the woodlands, how would we live without the mines?'

'You could trade with Tamrak's people or perhaps with the Vaane on the Lonely Isle. Both have an inordinate hunger for gems and minerals.'

Zara leaned forward. She swallowed, her voice nub bobbing. 'If you think ... I mean, if you promise to look after Jesson, my offer ...'

'No, child. This idea never made much sense. The Sea Dragon Kings are guilty of crimes, but would never have used such a wasteful and inefficient method of powering their mines.'

Nebam bristled. 'These are our mines.'

'Now they are and so they should be, for your ancestors built them.'

'How is it you know so much about our realm?' Havilah stood, her brow wrinkled.

Telsima tipped her head back and laughed, the musical notes echoing about the chamber with its pipes and machinery. 'We are not so different, we are all originally from the same blood lines. Even so, working with the crystals, being soul-bound to the ones of power. This all comes at a price. Which is why your people now live a mere couple of hundred years. But I say your people, for though I have inherited my mother's long years, my father came from this realm and I lived in the caverns as a youngwun.'

It was all fitting together. 'As Hezikah's father's playmate,' Zadeki said.

'The very same.'

Zadeki coughed. 'And Da-matu, that is when you learned the bat form.'

'Indeed. Now, maybe the injured need rest.'

A sensible suggestion though, as tired as he felt, he doubted he would. Adrenalin still buzzed in his veins, and he was hungry. 'I'll take first watch, if you like.'

Da-matu stood up and placed a hand on his arm. 'You did well, son of my son's son. One day soon, you'll make a fine pathfinder.'

Zadeki grinned, his hunger no longer important. He dropped to his knees and wrapped his arms around his da-matu and kinleader.

'Zadeki! Let me go!' She patted his shoulder as he released him. 'So young and eager. You did hear that I said, "one day."'

'Yes, Kinleader. And I can wait until you think me ready.'

Delvina lay awake, surrounded by the snores and sighs of the sleeping Darane, a littlewun crying and being hushed, the scrape of boot leather on the stone floor of a watcher on guard duty in the Grand Cavern. Her people. Where once, there would have barely been room to move when they were gathered together, now they had shrunk to two thirds the number and the glimmer lights had faded, casting a weak light that made the dark deeper around them. The cold stone floor was hard beneath her, disjointed thoughts raced through her head and her neck throbbed.

After all that effort, they were no closer to a permanent solution than before. It felt like being stuck in a tar pit. The greater their efforts of escape, the further stuck they became. Ferrying her people out on the backs of the shapeshifters in koraktil form would take many more rosters and then where would they go. From what she saw, her people could not survive in the forests and would be no use to the Vaane, who had valued them for their mining skills, if what Telsima said was true. Would the ones the Forest Folk called Tamrak's people welcome them, if they had mines to work?

'But ...' The words of the manual ran through her mind, 'Shepherd attune, heart vibrate'. Barekia said that the glimmer crystals' vibrations transmitted the power of the earth.

Her eyes drooped, her mind racing in half-dreams. Her head pounded and sweat dripped down her forehead. The wide world rushing toward her, the sick pallor of the glimmer lights, the sound of the Forest Folk singing in multiple harmonies, a bat with wide wings swooping toward her, the chant of words, the soft crackle of copper foil. Words buzzed in her head, attune ... song of field, forest and mountain ... true seed's blood ... blood lines.

She sat up suddenly, her neck lancing with pain. 'Blood lines.'

Retza stirred beside her and rolled onto his back. 'What?' He rubbed his eyes and yawned. 'Did you say something?'

'I couldn't sleep. I was thinking about the riddle.'

'What's the point, if we're not going to do what it suggests? Do you think we did the right thing? The Crystal Heart can't last much longer.'

'Do you mean saving Jesson and Zara? Yes, I do.'

'Okay, you don't have to jump down my throat. I can't help wondering about what Putarn said. Did we save two lives at the cost of so many?'

She glared at him. 'We're not dead yet, Retza. Zadeki and Telsima and the others, they'll help us.'

He sat up and gave her a shake. 'Yeah, but you could have died back there.'

'Ouch, I'm wounded, remember.' She chuckled then sobered. 'Why is my life more important than Zara's or Jesson's?'

'I don't know, Del. I don't want to think about losing you. We're a team, right? Yet, despite who her father is, Zara's a brave wun. I'm glad Telsima intervened when she did and you both got to live.'

She gave him a quick hug before he could protest and then poked his side. 'She is and a beauty. Some would say a good catch.'

'Oh, shut up.' He looked away, then back again. 'What did you say before ... something about blood lines?'

Did Retza have a soft spot for Uzza's daughter? Surely not.

'Delvina?'

She pushed the thought away, not sure what to make of it. 'I was thinking of the words of the codex, about whether 'ikor' or blood might have another meaning.'

Retza growled. 'I can't see how. I have nightmares thinking of our trek across the roof of the world to get such a useless answer.'

'But maybe it's not useless.' She scanned the Cavern. 'Where's Zadeki sleeping.'

'He offered to take first watch to guard the Heart Room with Josenif. Said he was too buzzed to sleep and besides, I think he planned to eat half those stores they brought. When he gets that hungry look, I get nervous.'

'Oh, that's right. But, he wouldn't eat us Retza.' Though he'd looked so fierce when he'd pounced on Javot. Shapeshifting did come with a price, much as using the crystals did, if Telsima was right. 'Come on. I have an idea.' Grabbing Retza's hand, she weaved her way through the sleeping bodies towards the Heart Room.

Delvina entered the room and scanned the perimeters. Havilah and Nebam were asleep beside Barekia's palette. The old Scrybe hadn't regained consciousness yet, but Telsima thought she'd live. Closer to the door, Gilarth sat beside Zara and Jesson, his chest wrapped in bandages, his head drooped forward in sleep. Uzza's children were not exactly prisoners anymore, but nor were they trusted, for who knew where their loyalties lay.

'I thought you two would be sleeping.'

Delvina jumped at Zadeki's voice. He was in his lanky

human form, handsome, dashing, maybe looking a little thinner.

She gripped his arm. 'Zadeki, where did the Kinleader say your power came from?'

'The song-lines of field, forest and mountain, we follow the Maker's song.'

'And the overseers are attuned to the crystals' song. Is that what soul-bond means?'

Retza's eyes lit up. 'Then maybe the crystals are attuned to the vibrations of the Overseer's heart.' He stopped and looked at Delvina. 'Though I'm not sure how that helps.'

Delvina nodded. 'Yes, that's it. Vibrations.' What if, 'in heart's tune' meant the vibration of the heart of the true seed.

She strode across the cavern and shook Zara's shoulder. Retza followed and stood behind her, his solid presence like ballast. The girl's eyelids flew open and she put up a defensive arm, drawing Jesson closer to her.

'What is it? What do you want?'

'I want to thank you, for being prepared to take my place.'

Zara's blue eyes darkened with suspicion. 'I was doing it for my brother.'

'We understand the bond.' Delvina and Retza spoke in unison and grinned at each other.

Delvina crouched down to their level. 'Can you do something for me? Can you touch the crystals?'

Retza moved closer. 'Didn't the Scrybe say not to touch them?

Delvina shook her head. 'Yes, because it puts them out of alignment, breaks the pattern in the vibrations. But don't you see, they are all but dead. We have to do something.'

Zara pushed herself up, rubbing the sleep out of her blue eyes. 'I'm not sure what I can do.'

Jesson took her hand. 'They helped us.'

Zara's face cleared. 'Yes, they did.' She glanced at the fading glow of the crystals. 'This doesn't involve blood, does it?'

'I hope not.' Zadeki looked from one to the other. 'Should we wake Havilah or speak to the Kinleader?'

'I don't want to raise hopes only to have them dashed again. But I think my idea will work.'

Delvina took Zara's soft hand and led her to the crystals on their central dais. A barrier prevented them from touching the crystals, no matter how high she tried to reach.

'Let me.' Zadeki picked Zara up by the waist and lifted her toward the biggest crystal that slanted toward them. 'Can you reach now.'

Zara looked mesmerised. She stretched out and laid both hands, palm down on the weakly pulsating light. Nothing happened.

'Hey, what are you youngwuns up to.' Barekia sat up, her eyes lucid.

Delvina smiled. That was one good thing. 'Solving the riddle.' At least she hoped so.

Zadeki hooted. 'You've decided to stay with us, Scrybe Barekia.' Though he kept holding Zara aloft.

Havilah startled awake, blinking the sleep out of her eyes.

'What are you youngwuns up to? Come away from there.' Havilah stood up in a rush, her hands fisted on her hips.

Gilarth roused and jumped to his feet, looking ready to rush them.

Delvina stepped forward. 'Please, your Honour. Just a few more minutes.'

Havilah frowned, then nodded. 'Perhaps, you've earned the right.'

Zara leaned in, wrapped her arms around the faceted surface of the dying Crystal Heart and hugged it.

Delvina's heart pounded a slow rhythm. She stared at the crystals, looking for the slightest change. Still nothing. Delvina slumped. She was so sure it would work.

'Thanks for trying, Zara.' Delvina turned to leave, when she felt a faint vibration under her boots.

A soft humming came from the long crystal, and was taken up by its neighbours. Bit by bit, the pulsating blue-green light grew in intensity. The stale air stirred and with a wumph the glimmer lights shone brighter, their blue fire reflected in Zadeki's, Jesson's and Zara's wondering eyes. Havilah stood beside Gilarth, a look of amazement on her face. The sound of cheering and laughter came echoing down the corridors from the Cavern.

Delvina clapped her hands. 'True heart's vibration. It is the living heart that revives the blood song of the crystal.'

Retza tipped his head back and gave a full bellied laugh. Something, she hadn't heard for a long time. Grabbing her hands, he twirled her around in a dance. 'We did it. You did it.'

Zadeki placed Zara on the ground, and Delvina ran over and pulled him down in a tight hug, feeling his strength. 'I knew you'd be able to help.'

'By the Maker's favour, I did little enough. We all had a part. Without you and Retza or Barekia and the Kinleader—'

'And Josenif and Gilarth.' Delvina let Zadeki go, and turned to where Uzza's children stood beneath the crystals, a mixture of relief and uncertainty in their eyes. 'And Zara and Jesson.' Delvina held out her hand, hardened from constant work. 'Without you, none of us could make the Crystal Heart work.'

Zara stood still, a hand on Jesson's head. She stepped toward Delvina and placed her soft hand in Delvina's calloused palm.

Delvina felt as though she was floating in a sea of blue light as the bright glimmer lights shone down on them. They'd done it and without the need to shed innocent blood. The revival of the Crystal Heart wouldn't solve all their problems, but it would give them time. Time to make plans and find other solutions.

And in all their troubles, they had made new allies against the fears and shadows, even those in their own hearts.

The End.

Acknowledgements

Blood Crystal is the sequel to *Heart of the Mountain*, continuing the adventures of the young shapeshifter Zadeki and the twins Retza and Delvina as the underground realm faces a desperate dilemma. The twins must confront their greatest fears and cross the mountains to search for their friend and answers to their problems. It's been a lot of fun to write and I appreciate my literary heroes like C. S. Lewis and J. R. R. Tolkien and so many others who fired my imagination as a child.

The events of this story occur many years after 'Ruhanna's Flight', but a few centuries before the events of the *Akrad's Legacy* series and the other *Tamrin Tales* (such as 'Fever', 'The Herbalist's Daughter' and 'Lakwi's Lament').

My heartfelt thanks to my wonderful editors, Nola Passmore (of *The Write Flourish*), and to my redoubtable critique partners and beta readers Kathleen Hillenberg, Paula Vince, and Suzanne Hay-Bartlem. Also, Julian Green, Nyssa Baschal, Rose Hill, Tjeila Mgueuene and others of the Intricate Worlds critique group.

I also had fun with the cover design, keeping the general design and tweaking the feel for this second story in the *Under the Mountain* series. I appreciated the critiques and feedback from the Omega Writers Science-Fiction and Fantasy Group.

I'm especially grateful for my family—my loving husband Tony, my precious children Kathleen and David, my parents Tom and Jean Curtis—who instilled in me a love of faith and fantasy—and siblings, Tom Curtis,

Frank Curtis, Chris Curtis and Kathleen Hillenberg, with whom I've shared many wonderful adventures.

As always, I'm grateful to my Maker in whose creative and imaginative footsteps I can only hope to follow.

Jeanette O'Hagan, June 2017

About the Author

Jeanette O'Hagan first spun tales in the world of Nardva at the age of eight or nine. She enjoys writing fiction, poetry, blogging and editing.

She is writing her *Akrad's Legacy* Series—a Young Adult secondary world fantasy fiction with adventure, courtly intrigue and romantic elements. Recent publications include novellas - *Heart of the Mountain* - and short stories - *The Herbalist's Daughter* and *Lakwi's Lament*. Other short stories and poems are published in a number of anthologies including *Glimpses of Light*, *Another Time Another Place* and *Like a Girl*.

Jeanette has practised medicine, studied communication, history, theology and a Master of Arts (Writing). She loves reading, painting, travel, catching up for coffee with friends, pondering the meaning of life and communicating God's great love. She lives in Brisbane with her husband and children.

Check out the social media of your choice—though Jeanette is most active on *Facebook, Twitter, GoodReads, Pinterest* and *Instagram*—and *Amazon Central* has all her books in one place.

Links and updates can be found at her website *Jeanette O'Hagan Writes* http://jeanetteohagan.com

or her email newsletter http://eepurl.com/bbLJKT

Author Note

If you've enjoyed this story from the world of Nardva, why not leave a fair and honest review on *Amazon, Goodreads* and/or your favourite reviewing site.

Writing reviews (no matter how short), helps support authors to keep on creating and publishing the stories you enjoy.

Coming Soon

Stone of the Sea – book 3 in the Under the Mountain series
Raesl's Song – book 2 of *Akrad's Legacy* series

Heart of the Mountain: a novella

YA Fantasy Adventure in the lost realm deep under the mountain.

Twins Delvina and Retza's greatest desire is to be accepted as prentices by their parents' old crew when they stumble across a stranger.

Trapped under the mountain, young Zadeki's only thought is to escape home to his kin.

Peril awaits all three youngsters. Will they pull apart or work together to save the underground realm?

Heart of the Mountain is the first novella in the Under the Mountain series. Set in the world of Nardva.

Amazon: https://www.amazon.com/dp/B01J74G9I6/
Elsewhere: https://www.books2read.com/u/4jMrvm

Ruhanna's Flight and other Stories

Ruhanna's Flight and other stories includes previously pubished and brand new stories set in the world of Nardva. A delightful introduction to Jeanette O'Hagan's fantasy world of engaging characters and stirring adventures.

> *"This author has the gift of immersing a reader in a different world and caring about the people in the world."* Amazon Review.

Now Available

Akrad's Children

Caught between two cultures, a pawn in a deadly power struggle, Dinnis longs for the day his father will rescue him and his sister from the sorcerer Akrad's clutches. But things don't turn out how Dinnis imagines and his father betrays him. Will he seek revenge for wrongs like his sister or forge a different destiny?

Akrad's Children is the first book in the Akrad's Legacy series

Now Available